the involuntary sojourner

the involuntary sojourner

STORIES

S. P. TENHOFF

Seven Stories Press
New York • Oakland • London

Seven Stories Press
140 Watts Street
New York, NY 10013
www.sevenstories.com

Library of Congress Cataloging-in-Publication Data

Names: Tenhoff, S. P., author.
Title: The involuntary sojourner : stories / S.P. Tenhoff.
Identifiers: LCCN 2019023453 (print) | LCCN 2019023454 (ebook) | ISBN
    9781609809645 (paperback) | ISBN 9781609809652 (ebk)
Classification: LCC PS3620.E546 A6 2019 (print) | LCC PS3620.E546 (ebook)
    | DDC 813/.6--dc23
LC record available at https://lccn.loc.gov/2019023453
LC ebook record available at https://lccn.loc.gov/2019023454

College professors and high school and middle school teachers can order free examination copies of Seven Stories Press titles. To order, visit www.sevenstories.com, or send fax on school letterhead to 212-226-1411.

Printed in the USA.

9 8 7 6 5 4 3 2 1

ACKNOWLEDGMENTS
The following stories previously appeared, sometimes in slightly different form, in the follow-ing publications: "Ten Views of the Border," *American Short Fiction*; "Maseru Casaba 9," *The Antioch Review*; "Liability," *Swink* and *Electric Literature's Recommended Reading*; "The Vis-itors," *The Gettysburg Review*; "Winter Crane," *Fiction International*; "Diorama: Retirement Party, White Plains, 1997," *Conjunctions*; "Ichiban," *Confrontation* and *Sequestrum*; "The Book of Explorers" and "Kurobe and the Secrets of Puppetry," *The Southern Review*; "The Involuntary Sojourner: A Case Study," *Conjunctions'* online magazine.

For W.

Contents

Ten Views of the Border

The imposition of borders was met, initially, with something akin to relief. This isn't to say that the citizens of the region were pleased at the prospect of seeing their familiar world dismantled before their eyes, but the period leading up to the imposition had been, let us not forget, pestered by rumor and anxiety. Now at least matters had been decided, and there was a general hope on the part of both the Northwestern and Southeastern Inhabitants (strange to hear ourselves described this way!) that life would return to normal.

But what was normal now? The respective governments issued a joint statement: "Northwestern Inhabitants (hereafter NWI) and Southeastern Inhabitants (hereafter SEI) are encouraged to pursue ordinary daily activities subject to minor alterations in keeping with the new regulations as listed below." No one read these regulations. Not at first. Or, rather, those who did found them a source of amusement, to be read aloud at dinner parties attended by NWI and SEI, still mingling freely, pointing and laughing at the colored bracelets as if they were part of a deliciously absurd new party game.

❋   ❋   ❋

Oskar Leong-Burke, born Year 2, NWI by birth, SEI by parentage, endured taunting with dignity from the earliest age. Secret pride, never acknowledged, may already have begun scraping out a cavity for itself by his shirttail-nibbling preschool days. Or his famous reserve might just as well have been a character trait utterly divorced from the events in his life. Try to sort these things out, try to trace bloom to root, and see how far you get. We know he never formally complained. No mention of his peculiar circumstances appears in his speeches, as if he found speaking of the matter beneath his dignity. (Again, dignity!) In any event, there was no need for him to mention those circumstances, as they were well known: the soon-to-be-father's midnight rush to a Southeastern hospital; the pneumatic hiss of his wife's breathing in the backseat. The necessary obstruction: either construction work or downed power line, depending on the version you favor. The rush in the opposite direction. The (ultimately venerated, initially reprimanded) border guard's permission to cross. The hissing. The winding road. The Northwestern hospital. The moans. The confusion: Parent 1 and Parent 2? Southeastern Inhabitants. Birth location? Northwestern Administrative Region.

❊   ❊   ❊

Obviously constructing a wall was impractical from the start. The general terrain of the region was not amenable. And the town itself—now the two towns—could hardly be split like a halved orange. The division, it was announced, should be conceived primarily as a state of mind. We were asked to regard the stripe across the town's belly, garish as a new tattoo, the way we might a symbol. Whereas the gates on the main roads, the border patrols, the weapons—all of this we were encouraged to view as something other than symbolic.

The home of Willetta Clum-Edbril, bordering as it did the park and therefore a patch of land neither side was willing to relinquish, became a point of contention. Half of her home was now in the Northwestern Administrative Region, half in the Southeastern; but as she refused to consider relocation, in spite of reasonable offers from both governments, the new line was, in the end, painted up one wall, across the roof, and down the other wall. Dual citizenship having been disallowed, the question of Willetta Clum-Edbril's status resulted in the determination that she would be awarded alternating citizenship: when in the Northwestern half of her home, she would be an NWI; when in the other half, an SEI. Since her front door offered egress to one region and her back door the other, it was only a matter of being certain to wear the appropriate bracelet before going out.

❀   ❀   ❀

But I remember him coming in the border patrol truck every morning. Like they were bringing some famous criminal. Him getting out. Every day it was like it was his first day there. The look on his face, I mean. Creepy. I shouldn't say that. But I mean. The teasing or bullying, I never took part in all that, but I can say, it sounds defensive or you know like apologizing or something for the behavior, but I don't think it was because of his coming from the other side. That was just the excuse. It was the look on his face. I mean if he didn't want to join in, then go play in a corner. Okay. Go play by yourself. But to just sit there at the edge of the playground and watch us all like that . . . Never a smile. It sounds like a blame-the-victim sort of, that kind of unfair sort of thing. But you didn't see his face.

❀   ❀   ❀

Each of the respective governments organized a contest to create an imagined history explaining the border for future generations. By a coincidence perhaps not so remarkable when you consider that we had, after all, until very recently been neighbors and fellow countrymen, both winning entries centered on the park.

The Northwestern entry reimagined it as the locus—the "historic heart," to quote the essay—of Northwestern regional pride and identity. Southeastern usurpation of the park (described as thrillingly as a barbarian invasion in an adventure story) leads to the inevitable conflict which ends in the establishment of a border. The other winning entry is as easily summarized: simply transpose in the above description the words "Northwestern" and "Southeastern."

From what can be surmised, the park had in fact nothing to do with the reason for establishing the border (whatever that reason was), but it invoked, for citizens of both sides, memories of lazy leaf-shaded afternoons and picnics pleasantly disrupted by carousing off-leash dogs and fishing for nonexistent fish on the green-slimed steps of Muck Pond, so it was easy to convert this genuine nostalgia into a foundation upon which might be built the new history we were expected to pass on to our children.

❀   ❀   ❀

But did little Oskar cry? No. He missed his father and mother just like you would, and the place called the relocation center was not a happy place, but little Oskar was brave. At night he looked out the window. And he thought of life on the other side of the border . . .

(In the accompanying black-and-white illustration, a barred oblong of moonlight stretches through darkness across a bare floor to an institutional cot, where it frames a boy, his tangled hair another patch of darkness. He is sitting up perfectly straight on the mattress, back and legs describing anatomically improbable right angles, staring toward the barred window although the look on his face is a listening look, as if he's hearing something we can't . . .)

❀   ❀   ❀

As in a landmark? No, the park was never—

It was just a park. What do you want from a park?

Although we do have a landmark as a matter of fact. Nothing all that remarkable about it, though, I wouldn't think.

Except that it's the oldest barn in the region.

Battered but intact, you might say.

Yes, a monument to the old ways of building.

Or to traditional farm life.

Or to those things that bend and bow but manage to survive.

We don't visit it much. After all, it's a *barn*.

Although kids have been known to deface the walls.

Yes but otherwise it goes unnoticed by us for the most part.

✾ ✾ ✾

There was at one point a TV program about Willetta Clum-Edbril. Really more about Willetta Clum-Edbril's home, the inside of which was depicted as being bisected, like the outside, by a boundary line. A couch, a rug, the back of a perpetually sleeping Labrador: all were red-striped, and on either side of this stripe the ambience, the décor, even the pattern of the wallpaper were markedly different. Before crossing the line, the actress playing the part of Willetta Clum-Edbril would change bracelets, bathrobes, and slippers. This, one supposes, was meant to be funny. Naturally, none of us believed for a moment it was really anything like that. Those of us who actually knew her recall startled green eyes, the scent of fennel, and a fondness for hinges . . . In our imaginations, when we envision Willetta Clum-Edbril at home, we see her sweeping a floor unmarked by any dividing line. We have her cook palm fritters, a favorite local dish. We make her iron clothes. Ordinary things. Sometimes, in our imaginations, she is allowed to look through the window at the guarded and fenced-in park, but we require her to stay inside, where we need her; and if we do occasionally let her out we always make a point of looking away so we won't know which door she is using.

✾ ✾ ✾

The borderline as an Idea: it doesn't do much for us. We don't know what to do with it, this Idea. Those who endorse this view of the border make us feel slow-witted and literal. The fact is, for most of us, it's a line. Broad and red and blistered in places. Two-dimensional but unquestionably real as it veers and rolls over three-dimensional space. Children play along the line on either side; some dare themselves to leap across and back again. (Although never little Oskar Leong-Burke!) The authorities, or at least those who actually monitor the borders, are surprisingly tolerant of this behavior. The line is an inconvenience. There's the bakery with the cheese sticks you can no longer frequent. The shortcut turned long. Endless detours in fact. And of course the other part: the friends, the relatives, all of that. Work-related Day Visas have reportedly become harder to obtain. We curse the line openly. But we curse it as a painted line, not as an Idea. This is something we insist on.

❈   ❈   ❈

The parade.

We march through the town, following the border, half of us on this side, half on that. The governments, although notified well in advance, have declined either to prohibit or to permit the parade, and this lack of recognition, this official silence, is interpreted variously by those among us as a sign of success or of failure. No one has gathered to watch; no crowds waving from the curb, no children hoisted onto shoulders. People look over, though, as they walk along the sidewalk. Their faces turn to observe from cars. A few lean out of windows. It wouldn't necessarily be true to say that we are "regarded with suspicion." Anyway, we are regarded; and the optimistic among us call it a sign of success. No one seems to recognize the man in the yellow poncho marching with us. It is a hot October afternoon, still summery, humidity gone now but the sun as bright and cruel as ever. At various points along the way we are forced temporarily apart, by buildings, walls, other assorted obstacles. We split apart and re-form again, following the line. What is the derivation of the term "Indian summer"? The question percolates, it effervesces up and down the processional line, but no answer is forthcoming. It wouldn't necessarily be true to say that we are all completely satisfied with the parade thus far. Some of us might have expected more. From the parade? From ourselves? Some of us want to stop for a moment, to have a cool drink and to rest, even if that only means standing briefly in the gust of an air-conditioned doorway before resuming. This proposal is, ultimately, rejected. It is not possible to determine on which side of the line this rejection originated, or if it formed without respect to the line at all. We march on minus cool drinks, minus air-conditioning. There is no insurrection. The optimistic among us point to this as a sign of success. (The man in the yellow poncho reveals himself to be in the camp of the optimists.) We march on until we reach Willetta Clum-Edbril's house. We have decided that this should be our end point. It really is unseasonably hot. We stand in front of Willetta Clum-Edbril's house. Her curtains are drawn. Her hinges, a diverse collection dangling from eaves, windowsills, and shutters, creak in the breeze, the free flaps glinting and trembling like the wings of butterflies half-pinned to a board. Some of us observe for the first time that the borderline's red stripe does actually, just as we have always heard, continue up the wall of her house; does actually cross the roof. Presumably does continue down the other side. Beyond, the park.

We stand there, the halted parade. We stand there for as long as we can, and then, in a collective decision that surprises us by its spontaneity, by not seeming like a decision at all, we turn silently around and we walk—we march, we march—back the way we came.

Maseru Casaba 9

The American boy was fifteen minutes late, and Kazu was starting to wonder if he'd gotten lost underground. From his car, Kazu scanned the heads that kept rising up out of Exit 4. Now and then blond appeared amid all the black, but each time it turned out to be another young Japanese with dyed hair.

It was his own fault: if he'd picked up his guest at the hotel, this would never have happened. Kazu had assumed that, since this was Jeremy's second visit to Tokyo, he would be able to navigate the subway system on his own. But he should have known a boy like Jeremy would end up having trouble. A teenage sleight-of-hand prodigy, he'd come three years before to lecture to a group of Japanese magicians, although "lecture" was hardly the word for what transpired: he'd gazed down impersonally at his hands throughout, transfixed by the actions taking place there as if the hands belonged to someone else. He hadn't even bothered to perform actual tricks; from start to finish, the show was an unapologetic display of card technique. His mute focus had made Kazu's job of interpreting nearly impossible. When prodded to explain a sleight, Jeremy would blink up at Kazu, then shrug, mumbling a few words Kazu could barely understand. It hadn't mattered, in the end: the audience was there to witness a phenomenon, not to pretend they could duplicate the wunderkind's feats. Kazu had expected the adoring teenagers; what had surprised him was the number of older magicians present, laughing ruefully at this seventeen-year-old's mastery of moves that had eluded them after decades of patient mirror practice.

But even if the audience had seemed satisfied with this dour pantomime, Kazu, standing there uselessly, had felt humiliated. He was used to having expectant faces turn his way as he deciphered the foreigner's secrets for them. And that was one reason why he'd invited Jeremy to his home this time: to coax some explanations from him in advance, so Kazu would be ready for the new lecture the following day.

But where was he? Kazu scanned the exit again: people trudged grimly up and out, up and out, refugees being steadily expelled from a subterranean kingdom. Still no sign of him. Could he have taken another exit by mistake?

Kazu was debating a call to Jeremy's hotel when he spotted a yellow crown of ruffled hair—unmistakable this time— followed by the same narrow, sharply beaked face Kazu remembered from three years before. The expression there, though, seemed somehow different . . .

Kazu jumped out of the car. "Jeremy-san!" he cried, waving. "Over here!" (Kazu always added *san* after a name when speaking in English. During his year in the United States, there had been nothing more shameful to him than the sight of people from his country desperately aping the crude slang and backslapping jocularity they saw as typically American. He learned that Americans insisted on using given names—his magic mentor would repeat, almost angrily, "Call me Robert!" every time Kazu said "Mr. Ormea"—but he'd found himself unable to speak to those he respected without some sort of proper honorific, so he'd taken to adding *san*. He realized how strange it sounded, but he also noticed that people were charmed and amused by the exotic appellation; it confirmed, together with Kazu's nervous deference, their image of what Japanese ought to be like, and over the years it had become a trademark, part of a character played for his foreign guests when they came to Japan.)

"Welcome back! Please . . ." He held the passenger door open while Jeremy squeezed inside, then raced around and climbed behind the wheel. "How was your flight?" he asked as they pulled away from the curb. "It must have been very tiring."

"Actually I like long flights. Plenty of time to practice . . . Kazu," he said (pronouncing the name ka-ZOO), "did you go on a diet or something?"

"No, not . . . Recently I've been . . . under the weather."

"Oh. Hey, sorry to hear that. Feeling better?"

"Much better, thank you. The doctor said it might have been stress, from overwork."

In fact the doctor hadn't known the cause of his condition. When asked if anything had been worrying him, the only thing Kazu could think of was the book he'd been working on, a translation into Japanese of a mammoth English work on sleight of hand. "Well that's probably it, then," the doctor had told Kazu, and then his wife; but it was only a guess, and Kazu was reluctant to blame magic for the terrifying collapse. (Besides, the two-year project was nearly finished. Why would he be experiencing anxiety now?) Whatever the cause, it had been an ordeal. He'd thought at first it might be the flu. Lethargy, headaches, a desire to stay curled up in bed under the covers . . . He couldn't think clearly; he couldn't work. The world receded, but at the same time he'd felt an excruciating raw sensitivity: light, sound, even his favorite music—every stimulus had become a spear. He spent days sealed in his room, where he wouldn't have to face his wife or son. For the first time in his life he didn't want to read books on magic; he didn't want to practice or even think about it . . . The medication the doctor prescribed seemed to help; it made him less anxious, at least, about whatever was happening to him. The doctor told him this was a sign of recovery. Even now, though, he at times found himself moving tentatively, as if housing a fragile, spiked object in danger of shattering at any moment . . .

"Well," Jeremy was saying, "at least you lost some weight, right? You look good, man!"

Which meant what? That there had been something wrong with the way he looked before? To change the subject Kazu said: "Could you, ah, find your way here all right? The Tokyo subway system is very difficult for foreigners, I think. Even Japanese—"

"Oh, no problem. Until I got here: I step off the train, and it's like: I can't tell if I'm in a subway station or a shopping center. No exits, stores everywhere, people rushing around . . . Pretty amazing."

"Ah yes, the station is connected to a department store. Very famous. You can find anything there. Even magic tricks."

All magicians, in Kazu's experience, had a story about how they'd first been "bitten by the magic bug." And Kazu had told his own story so many times he'd become an expert at the telling. When he was eleven, shopping with his mother at this same department store, he'd passed a magic counter. Inside the glass case sparkly cylinders, rainbow ribbons, and silver rings were arrayed in a shimmering display. The demonstrator suddenly handed him something: a red ball, the size of a marble. Kazu was told to drop it into a little plastic box on the counter. Then to put the lid on. Then to snap his fingers. The man smiled, removed the lid, and . . . the ball was gone. That moment was the first time in his life Kazu had felt genuine wonder. He'd bought the trick, of course, and later another, and another; and his life in magic had grown out of the desire to share with others the wonder he'd experienced that first day at the department store . . .

"I can't say I ever felt that," Jeremy said when Kazu had finished. "Wonder, I mean. I saw something on TV and thought it was kind of cool, so I went to the library and found a book. *The Expert at the Card Table.* That's how it started. The language was so old-fashioned, I could barely read it. I liked the diagrams of the hands, though. Very sort of clean and . . . clinical, you know. Like a manual. Then I realized how much I liked practicing. Not performing, just practicing. It could have been guitar playing or whatever. It just happened to be magic."

"Well. I must say congratulations."

He felt Jeremy looking at him.

"On your download."

When they first met, Jeremy had been largely unknown beyond the arcane world of technical card work; now it seemed that everyone in the magic community knew his name. This sudden fame was the result of a single trick, performed and explained by Jeremy on a downloadable video. From what Kazu could gather, his current lecture tour was mainly an excuse to promote the download, available on one of those websites featuring tricks with names like "Destruction" by scowling young magicians garlanded in chains and tattoos, the entire package designed to convince adolescent males that card magic could be cool, cutting-edge, even dangerous, like some kind of extreme sport. Jeremy's own trick was typical of this new brand of magic: brief, striking, and ultimately pointless—a flare shot randomly into a night sky. Magic reduced to the length and depth of a TV commercial, aimed at audiences with stunted attention spans. Kazu was nonetheless unaccountably excited to see Jeremy again. He had met and sessioned with legends; there was certainly no reason to be awed by some flash-in-the-pan talent, or swayed by all of the inane web chatter surrounding him. He refused to believe he was starstruck. He was probably just looking forward to the chance to teach the boy a thing or two about what really mattered in magic. A way to pass on something of value to the next generation. For most of magic's history the means of transmitting secrets—from mentor to select student—had been as treasured and clandestine as the secrets themselves. Books were published, but crucial details and preferred variations were often held back, having been judged too good to be revealed. In the darkest booths of bars (it seemed to Kazu that most of the greatest magicians he'd known were alcoholics), in twenty-four-hour cafeterias, on hotel room carpets, cards elegantly spread over stains and cigarette burns, aging nondescript men passed along what really mattered to those they had judged worthy . . .

Kazu had proven his own worthiness over the course of a twenty-year career serving as interpreter for magic's most respected names when they lectured in Japan. He also acted as unofficial guide, taking his guests first to an extraordinary little yakisoba restaurant known only to locals, then on an exclusive tour of Tokyo magic shops, and, finally, to a crafts store, where the foreign magicians spent giddy hours rummaging through boxes of rare items destined to be reimagined as props and gimmicks. He could see how grateful they were to be shown a Tokyo they would otherwise never have known existed. And he was more than repaid for his efforts with the "real work": sleights, subtleties, and tips that had never seen print and were intended to remain *sub rosa*, all of it recorded by Kazu in crabbed detail in a notebook he shared with no one. Kazu was proud of his reputation as able guide and interpreter; but he was, above all, proud to be recognized among the cognoscenti as a discreet keeper of secrets. And so Kazu despised the way Jeremy's generation was transforming the art of magic into a commodity to be bought and sold and openly traded like anything else.

He was surprised, then, when Jeremy said:

"Yeah, it's pretty ridiculous, if you ask me. All this attention over one trick. I don't get it. Personally, I've never downloaded a trick in my life."

They'd reached Kazu's public housing block. He turned reluctantly into its maze of parking lots: he'd never invited a foreign guest to his home before, and this home was nothing to be proud of . . .

"Like I said, I read *books*," Jeremy was saying. "Always have. That's how I learned everything I know." Everything I know: coming from a twenty-year-old, the remark made Kazu want to smile. "Learning from a video—what does it lead to? A thousand clones out there, doing exactly the same thing, right down to the patter."

Kazu parked. "Besides," Jeremy continued as they walked along the path, "most of those tricks only look good from one angle: in front of a webcam. View it from anywhere else and it'll flash like crazy, exposing everything. I include my own trick."

Kazu laughed. This was exactly how he'd always felt about

these tricks intended to be "performed" for a camera from the safety of a bedroom by boys his son's age, boys whose voices hadn't even changed yet, the probably pimpled head out of frame, and the result then proudly revealed to the world on a YouTube screen followed by an inevitable barrage of brutal posts from other kids who couldn't do any better.

"Obviously, that makes it seem like I'm some kind of sellout. And I'm not going to pretend I didn't do it for the money."

"Ahh, here we are, Jeremy-san." They'd reached his building's battered elevator. "Please, please, after you."

He nodded, distracted, and stepped inside. "But the way I see it—I realize this sounds like pathetic self-justification, but here goes: that download I made was full of proper crediting. Every last move. Something I insisted on. I had to fight to get it included, but my feeling was it might encourage some of the kids who watch these things to turn off the computer, pick up a book, and *discover* something. You know?"

"Mmm, yes," Kazu said absently as he took out his keys. He was thinking about his apartment, shabby even after the thorough cleaning he and his wife had carried out to prepare for their guest's visit. But more than the apartment, it was Mariko herself that worried him. He had made it clear that she was not to speak to Jeremy in English. Although she and Kazu had been English majors together in college, she hadn't spoken the language since graduating, and he could only imagine what her skills must be like after all this time. She'd been instructed to let him translate if she had anything to say; this way there would be no chance of her embarrassing herself. In any case, he and Jeremy would be busy with their session, and she wouldn't need to do much beyond providing refreshments. Still, he couldn't help but feel a little nervous . . .

"Please, come in," Kazu said, slipping his shoes off. He was relieved to see that Jeremy knew enough to follow suit. In the kitchen, Mariko was at work on a cake. She stopped and quickly wiped her hands on her apron, ready for a handshake. But Jeremy had already started jerking his head floorward in a clumsy bow; changing his mind, he straightened, waved vaguely, and said: "Hi . . . Sorry to barge in and, you know, steal your husband for the afternoon."

"No, Jeremy-san, no need to apologize," Kazu said. "She's used to it. My Japanese magic friends, they come over all the time. Sometimes our sessions go on so late they end up staying overnight!"

"Oh, right. A magic widow." The term—which Kazu had always hated—was a common joke among magicians, referring to the way wives were "widowed" by their husbands' lifelong obsession. "You have my condolences," he said to Mariko, smiling.

"He apologizes for intruding," Kazu said to her in Japanese.

She smiled back at Jeremy. "Tell him to make himself at home."

In the living room, Kazu had already placed two cushions on the mat, and on the coffee table two fresh packs of cards. But Jeremy, sinking cross-legged onto a cushion, immediately produced his own deck and began a series of intricate cuts, shuffles, and flourishes.

"Wonderful, Jeremy-san!"

Jeremy paid no attention. These, Kazu realized, were merely his warm-up exercises.

Mariko brought in tea. "Ask our guest if he likes chocolate cake," she said as she set down the cups.

"My wife is wondering if you like chocolate cake. Her hobby is baking desserts."

Jeremy squared the cards precisely on the table. "Yeah? Oh, I love pretty much anything sweet, so: yeah." He offered her a shy thumbs-up.

"What a relief!" she said to Kazu. "Tell him how happy I am. How I can't make sweets these days because of your diet."

"You can make sweets. I've told you that. It's okay once in a while for me to eat something I actually like. Besides, today's a special occasion."

Ever since his collapse, Mariko had been strictly regulating his fat and sugar intake. When the doctor first suggested a change in diet, she'd taken it personally, grumbling about what she saw as criticism of her cooking, but she'd also partly blamed herself for her husband's condition, and set about modifying the dishes she prepared. Kazu, at the time, didn't even notice. He was barely eating anyway, his appetite for food gone along with his appetite for everything else he loved. It was only after he started feeling better that he became aware of how scrupulously his favorite foods had been excised from every meal. When he looked in the mirror he barely recognized himself now. He might have been a bit ample before, but there had been color in his cheeks; he'd looked hearty and well fed. Now he was gaunt, insubstantial, pale skin draped sagging across bones like oversized clothes. It was that much worse, therefore, when his father-in-law clapped his hands delightedly at the sight of the new Kazu, his mother-in-law exclaiming with a wicked laugh that he looked handsome for the first time since she'd met him. This made him want to immediately devour a deep-fried pork cutlet with an ice cream sundae for dessert . . . Ever since their engagement, Mariko's parents had opposed her marriage to what they saw as an eccentric amateur magician barely making ends meets with his obscure translation work. Mariko had stood by him over the years, only complaining when his magic purchases got out of hand; recently, though, she'd been dropping comments about how they needed to start considering their son's college education, just four years away, not to mention their own eventual retirement. His work, translating instantly-out-of-print books for a handful of magicians, was simply not bringing in enough, even when supplemented by his part-time job at a bookstore. And so the way she'd beamed at her parents' reaction to the transformed Kazu had felt like a betrayal, like she'd finally joined with them in rejecting the man she'd married, favoring instead this underfed successor. As he recovered, Kazu had wanted nothing more than to return to his old self; but Mariko kept going on about how good he looked, as if hoping that with his new, stripped-down frame would come a new husband and a new life. She wasn't so brazen as to openly suggest that he change careers, but she'd begun using the doctor's words against him: his lifestyle had been unhealthy, she would say; this might be the perfect time to make changes for the better . . .

"I can have cake," he said with finality to her stony face, trying at the same time to keep his voice neutral so that Jeremy wouldn't think anything was amiss.

"Shall we begin, Jeremy-san?"

As Jeremy went over the tricks in his new lecture, the first thing Kazu noticed was that there was no gazing at the hands this time; he used misdirection now, executing moves while looking elsewhere. Kazu played the part of an ideal audience member, gasping and applauding at all of the appropriate moments. He knew what Jeremy was doing, of course: the sleights might have been impeccable, and the presentations diverting, but each time Kazu's keen gaze burned through it all to the essential structure, as conspicuous to him as the charred frame of a house on fire. Kazu had seen and read so much magic by this point in his life that he was nearly impossible to fool. So when he dutifully noted down Jeremy's explanations, his murmurs of appreciation—"Oh, I see; yes; now *that's* clever!"—were mostly a courtesy; nevertheless, the methods *were* often ingenious, and Kazu had to admire the boy's imagination.

Long after he'd finished with the material scheduled for the lecture, Jeremy was still going strong: trick after trick after trick . . . But when would Kazu have *his* chance? He was impatient to perform—it would be the first time since his illness. During a session, taking turns was standard etiquette: each magician might try to outdo the other, but always while respecting the fundamental balance of back-and-forth. Jeremy, though, seemed prepared to go on all afternoon. Which wasn't to say that Kazu found it all boring. There was no question that Jeremy had grown as a performer: the daunting sleights were still in evidence, but judiciously embedded now in complete routines; and while there was still something missing in his performances—he attempted suave polish, for instance, when what you wanted from someone his age was playful enthusiasm—this was nevertheless a far cry from the disturbing introvert of three years before. Kazu began to feel that the pieces he'd chosen to show Jeremy that day, solid tricks culled from his library, were pedestrian and overfamiliar. They had been intended as object lessons in how even the simplest magic could be effective if one focused on presentation. This was something he'd learned during his year in America, ostensibly there to continue his English studies after college, but really on a pilgrimage to meet the great Robert Ormea. Under his tutelage, Kazu had come to recognize that skill was only part of any successful performance, and that a magician was almost always better off concealing rather than flaunting it. "Don't forget," Robert was fond of saying, "basically, when all is said and done, people do not like magic. Who can blame them? Nobody likes being made to feel stupid. They have to be fooled into enjoying being fooled. And that's where entertainment comes in." Kazu had hoped to pass this wisdom on to Jeremy; but since they'd last met, Jeremy had obviously managed to figure it out for himself. So what should Kazu show? After all of this boy's inventiveness, it was embarrassing to think that he had nothing of his own to offer; but Kazu's magical gifts had always been critical rather than creative. Whatever he showed, it needed to be something special, something Jeremy wouldn't already have seen . . .

"Jeremy-san, have you heard of the FBC?" he blurted, to his own surprise.

"FBC. What's it stand for?"

"FBC is—Well, first, first I should explain how— It's an amazing story, Jeremy-san! I'm sure you know Robert Ormea?"

"The name."

"Yes well he was my mentor! I saw him this year, at a magic convention in New York. Afterward, he said he had a surprise for me. And then he drove me to—Jeremy-san, can you imagine where?"

Kazu paused.

"Poughkeepsie."

Jeremy lifted empty hands and shrugged them apart in either puzzlement or indifference.

"Oh. You don't know who lives in Poughkeepsie, Jeremy-san? A very famous name in magic. A *legend* . . ."

When it became clear that Jeremy had no intention of

guessing, Kazu slowly revealed the name. He waited for a reaction.

". . . Do you know who he is?" he asked finally.

"I've heard of him. I didn't realize he was still alive."

Still alive? How disrespectful! Although there was no denying it: Feinmann *was* getting on. Kazu had been taken aback when the front door opened . . . The figure there, alarmingly frail, steadied itself on the doorframe. This was Harold Feinmann? After the introductions, they followed him inside. He seemed alert, at least, if milder and less acerbic than his reputation suggested; possibly Robert had vouched for Kazu in advance. He was actually wearing the fabled gloves! The gloves worn constantly to keep the fingertips moisturized for card work, to protect the hands—belonging to a retired postal worker, of all things—that had been called the greatest in magic. In a loud but gentle voice, Robert asked Feinmann if he could show Kazu his FBC. The Flexible Block Control was a move that, in its very absence from the published record (and even conjectured nonexistence), had achieved the status of myth. (Of course, nearly *all* of Feinmann's work was unpublished. He was notorious for hoarding his methods, ever since a magician put one of Feinmann's sleights into print under his own name. He seemed prepared to take his discoveries to the grave with him. Perhaps no name in magic had been built so purely on rumor and withheld information.) Feinmann slid off one glove, then the other. The hands, revealed: ordinary in size, narrow-fingered, complexly veined and spotted. They cradled a deck and did . . . nothing, apparently; until he raised them to expose for Kazu the serene clockwork shifting and realignment of cards . . . And then he painstakingly explained what his fingers were doing, as if

Kazu had been designated the one meant to ensure that the move would not be lost forever.

Kazu had practiced it for months, and had reached the point where—judging from the view in his practice mirror at least—the move might be nearly passable; but then his illness had struck, and he hadn't practiced it or any other demanding sleights since . . .

He rose up onto his knees and took a deck in his damp hands. He ordered the hands to stop shaking.

"Feinmann's Flexible Block Control: would you like to see it?" he asked; and without waiting for an answer, executed the move.

". . . How did it look, Jeremy-san?"

". . . Oh, my angle here wasn't so good. I was a little below you, which wouldn't normally—"

"Did I flash?"

"A little. But I can imagine, you know, how it should look . . ."

"Yes, I'm sorry, I should have practiced more, it still needs work. I can't perform it yet, but maybe I can demonstrate . . ."

Jeremy, though, had already picked up his own cards and, cradling them gently, did . . . nothing.

"Like that?"

"Perfect, Jeremy-san! Perfect!" Kazu cried, voice bright with lavish enthusiasm to hide his desolation.

"Really? It's a beautiful move. It should be more well-known. Have you got a mirror?"

"Ah. Yes, one moment please, I'll bring—but one thing, Jeremy-san. Please don't show this to anyone. I promised I wouldn't—"

"Oh, yeah, of course."

Kazu already regretted sharing the move. Why had he done it? How did he know Jeremy wouldn't show the FBC to every young magician he met? Soon there would be a video tutorial on the internet and both Robert and Feinmann would know that Kazu had given away the secret . . .

"The mirror?"

"Right!" He hurried to his feet. "Sorry!"

In the kitchen, Mariko stood at the sink, washing dishes. The cake was in the oven, baking in its square of light. He passed through the warm smell—a smell so rich and promising he momentarily forgot his guilt. Chocolate: today would be his first time in . . . Weeks? No; longer . . . The smell! It was like the promise of celebration. After everything he'd endured since his collapse. The celebration of a return to himself . . .

It took longer than expected to find his practice mirror. He knew it must be there somewhere, hidden among all the things relegated to the study when they cleaned up for Jeremy's visit. He'd always kept his magic materials—the books, the periodicals, the monographs and lecture notes—within arm's reach throughout the apartment, and although Mariko called it chaos everything was in fact stacked and separated according to a private system—he could locate an item instantly if he needed to. At first he'd tried to maintain the system when they started moving the piles, but Mariko had practically thrown whatever she found into the study—"I feel like I've finally gotten my apartment back!" she'd said exultantly when they finished—and now it was all a sad jumble, order destroyed, everything abandoned here in a ruin of collapsed walls, broken arches, and teetering columns . . .

The mirror was buried under a heap of old magazines. Kazu hurried back with it, back through the kitchen's warm birthday smell, to the living room, where Jeremy sat still cradling the deck in his hands. Kazu placed the mirror on the table before him, opened the side panels, and sat down to wait while Jeremy began performing for himself, disregarding Kazu completely. Should he repeat the importance of keeping the move a secret? Would repeating it even matter now?

Something blurred past his shoulder. It arced and dove, a bluish something, arced again and, alighting on the bookshelf, quivered into a stable shape: a bird, alive and red-chested . . .

"Ah! Mariko!" Kazu rose, stumbled toward it, stumbled away. "Mariko! A bird! A bird got—"

Mariko rushed in, vanished, and reappeared with a broom.

"Jeremy-san," Kazu began, "I'm sorry—"

It whirred by, struck the lamp, started a twirling fall and looped up toward the ceiling.

"Kazu, out of the way!" Mariko cried, raising the broom. Kazu felt light-headed and sluggish, unable to move . . .

"Wait, don't hit it!" Jeremy shouted, leaping up, both hands extended, as if to cup the creature between them.

"No, Jeremy-san, it's okay, let—"

Something—a wing tip? a current of air?—brushed his ear. Mariko barreled past, broom swinging.

In English, in Japanese:

"It's okay, don't—"

"Hold on—"

"Where is it?"

"—it go?"

"Do you see it?"

"Wait, let's—" Kazu held up his hands weakly as if to ward off attacks coming from all sides. "Please, let's . . ." He half sat, half collapsed onto the tatami mat. "It's gone," he said, eyes closed, unsure if this was in fact true.

"Must've flown back out the window," Jeremy said.

"Ahh," Mariko laughed, elated. To Kazu she giggled: "Did he think he was going to catch it bare-handed? Funny kid . . . Tell him I wasn't going to hit it. He'll think I'm some sort of . . ." She carried the broom back into the kitchen. "How did he think he was going to catch it?" her voice went on. "Even magicians' hands aren't that fast." He heard her laughing at her own joke.

Kazu felt drained. His sickness—perhaps he wasn't completely recovered after all . . . Finally he thought to get up and close the door to the balcony. "I'm sorry, Jeremy-san," he said. "I should have kept this closed. We're very high up here, eleventh floor, and—"

"No, hey, no problem. A little excitement."

"Tell him," Mariko repeated from the doorway, not laughing anymore. "I don't want him to think I'd hurt a bird."

"Yes, yes, all right," Kazu said irritably. "My wife wants you to know she was only trying to scare it away."

"Well I think it worked." Grinning at her, Jeremy began flourishing an invisible broom. "Nice job!"

She in turn mimed cupping something between her palms.

Kazu heard them laughing together, each at the other. He had closed his eyes again. When he opened them, Jeremy had a piece of paper in his hand. He held it aloft.

"A prediction," he said solemnly; Kazu couldn't tell if he was being serious or mocking the self-important tones of the typical mind-reader. "This one I've never shown to anyone. This is just for you." He set the paper on the table.

"Ah, mentalism! I didn't know you performed mental magic, Jeremy-san. Later, later I must show you something, I think you'll like it. Do you know 'The Inopportune Prediction' by Philip Van Balkom? A very good friend, he—"

"No. Kazu, this is what I want you to do." He still had the solemn tone. Now it didn't seem like a joke at all. Kazu found it annoying, but put on an earnest face and waited to be commanded.

"Name a city," Jeremy said, taking a pen and notepad from his pocket. "A city you'd like to visit."

Kazu knew all about the use of psychological influence and population stereotypes in mentalism; after all, he'd translated into Japanese a book by one of its foremost practitioners. (The author had even signed a copy for him.) The solution was to provide random information. Paris, Rome, possibly Honolulu: these would be the obvious choices. He tried to recall the capitals he'd been forced to memorize in his high school geography class. Oslo? No: too well-known. Djibouti. Was that even a city? Then he remembered an African capital he and his classmates had joked about because the word was, coincidentally, pronounced just like the Japanese word for "precocious."

"Maseru," he said.

Jeremy frowned but jotted it down.

"Your favorite fruit?"

Was *pomegranate* obscure enough?

"Casaba," he said.

"A number from one to ten. Don't think about it too much; give me the first number that comes into your head."

Kazu ignored this. Seven, of course, was the most frequent response. But Jeremy would realize that Kazu already knew that. One and ten were too extreme, five too snugly balanced in the middle. He considered three. But maybe this was exactly what magicians, avoiding the most common choices, gravitated toward . . . He settled on eight and changed his mind.

"Nine."

Jeremy pretended to ponder the answers. He nodded to himself meaningfully. Kazu knew it was all nonsense, of course. Finally Jeremy put a finger to his lips, nodded once more and said:

"What I'm getting here"—he tapped the notepad—"is that you're at a crossroads in your life. You've recently started questioning whether the things you've placed value in are really of value. Does that make sense to you?" Kazu didn't answer. ". . . You push yourself very hard. You do everything to the best of your ability and people respect you for it. This respect is important to you. At the same time you sometimes wonder if you deserve it." Kazu wanted him to stop. He reminded himself that this was just stock cold reading, probably memorized straight from a book. "This could be wrong—it's ambiguous, but it seems to suggest that . . . It's not clear. Possibly that you've lost something important to you . . ."

He put the pen and notepad away. "But none of this is a surprise to me. Before I came here today, I had a feeling about you, Kazu. I wrote it down." He pointed at the prediction. "Take a look."

Kazu picked up the piece of paper. He unfolded it.

Maseru
Casaba
9

"Wait," he mumbled in Japanese. "Wait a minute." He set the paper down. When he picked it up again the words were still there.

Maseru, Casaba, 9 . . . The department store's magic counter appeared before him. And he suddenly remembered what he'd felt that first time, years before, when the lid was lifted and the ball was gone. It wasn't wonder. It was horror, horror at how *wrong* this impossibility was, horror followed by some species of despair, followed by fury: he'd wanted to take the box and smash it into the glass counter. What he bought that day, and the next time, and the next, what kept him coming back, was the desire to demolish that feeling by learning all of the secrets the world had to offer. He had told the false story of his first magical experience so many times he'd fooled himself, misremembering what he'd really felt when he looked into the box. In his life, he had never experienced *wonder* at all. Unless *wonder* meant that loathsome queasy feeling when, for an instant, common sense ceases to operate and nothing is what it's supposed to be . . .

"Are you ready for some cake?" his wife called from the doorway.

(In English: Kazu registered the language belatedly, with remote surprise.)

He stared at the paper as if waiting for the letters scrawled there to reorder themselves into an explanation for a lifetime without wonder.

(Jeremy and his wife, speaking to each other now, in English.)

Maseru Casaba 9: A lifetime without wonder . . .

"Okay, Kazu."

Kazu looked up. Jeremy had begun pulling things—the notepad, the pen—from his pocket. "I've kept you stewing long enough," he said, eager to show he wasn't the sort of magician who'd fool a brother in the fraternity and then gloat, sitting on the method, the way some would. "I guess you want me to tell you how it's done."

Kazu knew he was required to say yes, to beg this boy to

tear away the mystery and grant him one more secret for his notebook.

Mariko came in carrying the silver tray reserved for special occasions. It gleamed, newly polished.

"Sorry to interrupt," she said in English. "Here you are." She set the tray down. And Kazu was so grateful for the reprieve he could even forgive finding only one slice of cake there.

Liability

Doug hit the kid while he was driving home from his weekly chess game with Otto the liquor store clerk. He had lost the game in a humiliating reversal, after feeling sure he had Otto whipped using an obscure line of the Taimonov system found in an old *Chess Life.* Otto gloated, as usual. He went backwards for Doug, replacing pieces on the board, untangling positions, all the way to the point of the fateful blunder.

"Here's where your game went south," Otto said mournfully, his fingertip on a bishop's slotted head. "Right here."

The kid sped into the intersection on a mountain bike, straight through a red light, torso tilted down aerodynamically. The bike ended up half under his car and the kid ended up down the street. A guy and his dog came over and watched the kid twitch for a little while. Doug joined them.

"You got your phone?" the dog owner said. "'Cause I don't. Otherwise I'd call."

Doug took his phone out of his pocket.

"You want me to make the call for you? Can you handle this?"

"I'm fine," Doug said, handing the guy his phone.

There was no blood. The kid twitched. He looked maybe fourteen. The dog owner called 911 and gave their location and Doug's license plate number.

"She says don't touch him," the dog owner told him.

"I'm not going to touch him," Doug said.

The dog quit sniffing the kid and looked up at its master with a *let's get moving* kind of expression.

"She said five minutes if you can believe her," the dog owner said, returning his phone. "Don't touch him. Just leave him be."

"Right."

The kid wasn't moving anymore.

"Which, hell, we don't need her to tell us, right? What are we gonna do? Don't touch them. That's the first rule. Leave it to the professionals. 'Cause you could do more damage that way. Shifting things that are you know . . ."

"Right."

"Jesus Christ."

"He wasn't wearing a helmet."

"Jasper, sit."

An ambulance came, spraying the intersection with the sound and colors of panic. But the men who got out worked in an efficient way that calmed everything down. They worked very fast but without any apparent sense of urgency, reminding Doug of the pit-stop crews in professional auto racing. By the time the police arrived the paramedics had the kid strapped onto a stretcher and were putting him in the back of the ambulance. As they sealed him in and screamed away, all he could think was: Thank God for those guys! They were like a hazardous waste disposal unit. Or a bomb defusing squad. They were like a special cleanup team that removed impossible things from the intersections of the world.

❁   ❁   ❁

The police separated them: one talked to Doug and one talked to the dog owner.

Doug kept trying to listen to what the dog owner was saying. He could hear him make a whistling sound as he gestured with one hand.

The cop who was questioning Doug took his driver's license to the patrol car. After a minute he brought it back.

The other cop squatted and said something to the dog Jasper.

A car had stopped in the intersection. Inside, a little girl and a man with glasses watched the five of them. They weren't gaping, the way you imagine bystanders at an accident. They looked shrewd and knowing, like a pair of insurance investigators already on the scene. The cop who was talking to Jasper stood up and waved the car along.

"If asked, would you agree to a breath alcohol reading?"

Doug thought about this carefully. His answer to this question seemed crucial, even though he hadn't been drinking.

"Yes," he said finally.

Where was Jasper's owner? Where was Jasper? They were nowhere to be seen. Their cop was measuring the skid marks behind Doug's car with a tape measure. Doug's cop went to the patrol car again and came back with a black object in his hand. At first Doug thought it was a Breathalyzer kit, but it turned out to be an Instamatic camera, which he used to take a picture of the front of the car.

"That about does it," the cop said.

"What about the bike?" Doug said.

"Let's see if we can't yank her out of there."

Together they did yank it out of there. It made a scraping, wrenching sound which for no good reason made Doug think of a filling being ripped from an open mouth with a pair of rusty pliers.

That sound: it was the worst part of the whole ordeal.

They looked down at the bike. It wasn't mangled the way he had expected it to be. The handlebar was maybe twisted a little and the front wheel was shot but other than that the bike looked fine.

One cop opened the trunk and the other one fit it inside.

"Thanks," he said to them as they got in the patrol car. It didn't seem like the right thing to say.

He stood on the curb and watched them pull away. His cop lifted his fingers from the wheel in a little wave. As they drove off it occurred to Doug that he hadn't been given the Breathalyzer test.

❀ ❀ ❀

As soon as he got home he went over to check the answering machine. He stared down at the box's unblinking red eye, trying to decide whether he was relieved. He went into the living room, turned around, went back to the machine and turned it off.

For a while he watched TV. He didn't let himself drink yet. Postponing was a recent policy: he would make himself wait if it seemed like maybe he was about to drink because he needed to. For some reason he thought of his ex. He sat on the couch and waited to feel something about the accident. Emotional disconnectedness, he knew, is a symptom of shock. It often happens to people following a trauma. It's perfectly normal.

Finally he got up and rummaged through drawers until he found his insurance brochure. It was Sunday evening, but the brochure said "24-hour customer service 7 days a week" and gave a toll-free number. An automated voice led him through a cycle of choices, none of which pertained to his situation. He went in and out of submenus and ended up on the main menu again. When he refused to push a button or speak into the receiver the voice told him to hold for the next available customer service specialist. There was some music, a click, and then a different automated voice told him to call during regular business hours.

He wandered around their website for a while, not knowing where to look. Eventually he went to the SEARCH box and typed in the keywords

accident pedestrian injury coverage

then deleted

pedestrian

and replaced it with

cyclist

which he changed to

bicycle

but just before clicking GO! he hesitated. Finally he added the word

accidental

❋   ❋   ❋

He was on his second drink when the phone rang. He set the glass down and listened: seven complete rings, followed by an eighth strangled half-ring.

❋   ❋   ❋

He decided to take the bus to work the next morning. Here it was the end of October and people were still in short sleeves. Across the sky clouds were fraying like ten-minute-old jet contrails. Wind blew bright gusts of sunlight down the street. Cars stopped and started and turned and coursed along together, the parts to some elaborate windup toy, all moving in sync and no way for anything to go wrong.

He hadn't found what he was looking for on the website. After scrolling down a long page of print he'd realized that he was reading about cyclists' coverage in an accident with an automobile instead of the other way around. During lunch break he sat on a bench outside and called the company again. He again refused to choose a number or to speak into the receiver when prompted, and this time got a customer service specialist named Craig who asked him a series of questions to verify his identity and then told him that information regarding coverage couldn't be answered over the phone. Craig referred Doug to the website for more information. Doug told Craig he had tried the website. Craig said he would be happy to walk Doug through it. Doug said he wasn't in front of a computer. Craig suggested he call back when he was.

It was already dark when he left work. The windup cars coursed along, stopping and starting, their ends lit white, their ends lit red.

❧   ❧   ❧

He sat down in front of his chessboard. The pieces reenacted the situation after Black's quirky and decisive pawn sacrifice at move 13 of Kuzmin–Taimonov, Leningrad 1977. He tried to spend some time every evening moving through various lines. He had been doing this for about a year, ever since he started playing chess with Otto.

Doug had walked into his local liquor store one day and found Otto perched on a stool behind the counter. He looked vaguely reptilian. He was reading a paperback. Doug could see little chessboard squares and blocks of notation on the page. Otto didn't look up until Doug thumped his bottle down on the counter. Then he reluctantly tented the book and rang up Doug's order in a sort of patiently long-suffering way. Every time Doug went in Otto was either reading a chess book or staring at a little magnetic board he kept half-hidden behind the register. One day Doug leaned over, took a good look at the board, and said: "Who's winning?"

". . . What?"

"Are you black or white?"

"I'm both," he said. "I'm neither," he said. "I'm studying a position."

And then, when he saw Doug was still looking, Otto slid the board out from its hiding place for Doug to see.

After that they sometimes talked chess when Doug went in. Growing up he had been a good, if casual, player. People said he had a natural talent. When he set his bottle down Otto would slide the board from its place behind the register and make him guess the best move. If Doug picked the wrong one Otto would explain why it would be disastrous five or six or ten moves down the line. Doug realized later that Otto had been testing him. Finally Otto started inviting Doug to his house to play on Sunday afternoons. Losing was surprisingly painful (had he ever lost as a kid?), yet he found himself returning week after week. When he asked himself why, he decided it was his pride. Or the fact that the divorce had just been finalized, and time spent at Otto's place was time not spent alone. Besides, the evenings at home, planning his eventual victory—he educated himself on chess theory, tested strategies against a software program called "Grandmaster," searched through edition after fat edition of *Modern Chess Openings* for a magic formula—it all gave him something to do in the empty apartment besides drinking and brooding over things that were no longer supposed to matter.

Now Kuzmin–Taimonov provided him with the same kind of distraction from the accident: before he knew it three hours had passed without him thinking about it once. At the same time he had the sense that it might actually have been there in the back of his mind all along, like a chess problem you can't solve: you're beating Otto; somehow you fuck up again; for the next week, no matter what you're doing, a part of you keeps trying to figure out how it happened. Two pieces intersect: there's an unexpected outcome. The kid went straight through the intersection without even slowing down. Of course it wasn't a chess problem. A human life was involved. But was he a monster for trying to make sense of it, for trying to reduce it to something as clean as the pattern of squares on a board? The kid went straight through. Doug hit the brakes too late. Why turn it into something more complicated than that? What was there to do now but continue with his life, which meant, for the most part, sitting alone in front of the chessboard, postponing the evening's first drink, studying positions and imagining himself finally beating Otto?

❀   ❀   ❀

He was riding the bus to work the next morning when it occurred to him that maybe the story he'd told the police officer wasn't accurate. That maybe, once he saw the kid coming, he had accelerated before hitting the brakes.

❀   ❀   ❀

An insurance agent came to his apartment. He said he had been trying to contact Doug. He looked tired. He was the sort of man who looks rumpled even when he isn't. He had a copy of the police report. While looking down at his clipboard he read back the questions the police officer had asked. Doug repeated his answers. He learned the name of the kid he'd hit.

The kid had died, as it turned out. He hadn't made it to the hospital.

The insurance agent said Doug appeared to be covered through the bodily injury liability clause of his policy, but he advised him not to contact the family or to answer any questions if they or their lawyer contacted him. Then he gave Doug his business card.

The dog owner had corroborated his story: the kid raced straight into the intersection without even slowing down at the red light. That story still felt true. It just didn't feel complete. There was the part about Doug accelerating when he saw the kid. By now he was convinced he had hit the gas pedal and hit it deliberately, if that was the right word. He was pretty annoyed with Otto at the time, although he couldn't really say whether that had anything to do with it. It was just a split-second thing. Chances are he would have hit the kid anyway.

The scraping sound when the bike was pulled out from under his car.

He stayed where he was on the couch. Postpone. Postpone.

Something seemed to be wrong with him. He didn't seem to be able to feel anything about the kid's death. He tried different constructions: *If it weren't for me that kid would be alive today. A boy is dead because of me. My actions cost a kid his life.* And finally: *I killed someone.* He couldn't get the words to mean what they wanted to. They just sounded like words. Maybe he was in denial. Wasn't denial one of the stages in coping with death? But it didn't feel like that. It didn't feel like anything.

And then an emotion appeared: he started to feel guilty about not feeling guilty about what he'd done.

❊   ❊   ❊

He went into the liquor store. "I hit this kid," he told Otto.

"What kid?"

"With my car."

"When? Just now?"

"After our game. The kid died."

Otto gave him a free bottle of J&B.

He walked home. It was another warm night. Leaves shushed overhead. They looked yellow, but it was just the light from the sodium lamps: they were really still as green as ever. Really nothing had changed. It was fall but it wasn't fall. It would just go on and on like that, he realized—an endless unchanging season.

When he got back to his apartment he took the bottle out of

its paper bag, set it on the kitchen table, and stood there for a long time looking at it.

❀   ❀   ❀

He woke up and lay in bed trying to remember his dreams. Sometimes he could sort of feel his way around an outline, a shape, but there would be nothing inside it; all he could be sure of was that he'd been dreaming. Other times a scene would stay with him as he lay there, and he'd think it might be significant until he examined it, and found nothing but random scraps from his daily life all strung together in a row. He kept looking for the kid, or for the kid's bike. Then again, he thought, dreams don't usually come at you straight like that. So he searched for some transfigured sign of the accident; but he didn't dream of police, or traffic signals, or ambulances. He didn't dream of insurance agents or parents standing in his doorway with silent accusing faces. He didn't even dream of dogs.

❀   ❀   ❀

He started driving again. He drove more slowly than usual, both hands on the wheel. He wasn't afraid exactly. It was like he was waiting for something to happen—a revelation maybe— and he didn't want to rush past and miss it. One day after work he went through the intersection where he hit the kid. Not because he felt compelled to return there; it was on his way and he told himself he wasn't going to make a detour anymore just to avoid it. He stopped on red, waited until the light changed, drove slowly through. It was just an intersection. You couldn't tell by looking that anything had ever happened there.

He hadn't played Otto since the accident, but he still spent his evenings gazing down at Kuzmin–Taimonov, move 13. There were no revelations to be found there either. Chess, he finally decided—he was at the board late one night, a glass wavering over the squares like a piece in mid-move, his once-strict rule about mixing chess and alcohol abandoned now—chess is only revelatory when you don't understand it. In fact there are no secrets to the game: it's simply incremental, the gradual accretion of details that lead you in a certain direction, sealing off choices, one after another.

❀   ❀   ❀

He called the insurance agent and asked for the address of the kid's parents. The agent advised Doug again not to contact them. He had seen people jeopardize their coverage that way, just opening the door wide to liability. Finally, though, he read the address out for Doug, along with the father's name.

The place was less than a mile from his apartment. This made sense; after all, Doug and the kid had been using the same intersection. But the proximity of their homes seemed to have some kind of sinister significance. He was thinking he might have passed the house before, driven right by the place where the kid spent his life. The block turned out to be unfamiliar, though. Southeast Gladstone was a quiet street with small run-down houses on one side and a closed warehouse on the other. The Sekowsky home was the nicest one on the block: it had a fresh coat of paint at least, and a well-tended front yard.

The house was dark when he got there. He felt disappointed, depressed even, although during the whole drive over he had been terrified that someone might actually be home and he might have to go up to the door. He sat in his car and stared at the house, as if, by looking hard enough, he could make it blink to bright life, shadow-play figures set into sudden motion behind the curtains. Nothing happened. It was the same thing the next night, except, when Doug was about to give up and leave, a car pulled into the driveway.

❀   ❀   ❀

Raymond Sekowsky (if that's who it was) looked about Doug's age. He got out of an old Camry, a compact, deeply tanned man in a green work uniform. My age, Doug thought, and already a teenage son. He must have started early.

Or maybe it was just that Doug had started late. It wasn't his idea. His wife came out of the bathroom holding the test stick and told him, "No more abortions." So that was that: the baby was born. He'd tried to convince her he wasn't ready, wasn't fit for fatherhood. It didn't matter. The baby was born. It came out pissing. Like one of those plaster cupids. The arc barely missed Doug as it was moved from between Kim's legs to a complicated table nearby. Doug glimpsed a bluish-gray body. Over the nurse's shoulder, he saw the face for the first time: a purple fist, clenching and unclenching around its giant wail. Very impressive, that wail. It seemed intent on convincing him that this was all really happening. Doug was convinced. The fact of his fatherhood trembled there an arm's length away, pissing and wailing, purple and gray, furious and incontestably real.

Four days later the baby came home with them. Doug was stunned at the way it took for granted that it belonged there, that its cries were meant to be answered. Kim gave in immediately, serene and stoical in her exhaustion. She might not have been eager to sacrifice everything for the baby, but she seemed sure that she was doing exactly what she was supposed to. Doug would stare at it sometimes, at the enormous black alien eyes—where did *those* come from?—and the cheeks cross-hatched with the claw marks it inflicted on itself in its sleep. He would stare at his son, and suddenly feel terrified. What are you supposed to do with love like that? It wasn't reasonable. Neither was drinking all the time, but at least he got the feeling that he was making some kind of progress, that he was fortifying himself against that terrible love. He was already a drinker, of course, but this was different. This was like work. He threw himself into it. Kim said if he loved his son he should be able to stop. Which was *really* unreasonable. She couldn't understand what it was he was trying to accomplish. When she finally left, when she took his son away from him, he drank in weepy celebration. He forgave her—the bitch!—for abandoning him. He forgave her for having the baby. By taking it away, she was only trying to undo the wrong she had done to him. All in all, he was glad they were gone. Relieved. Grateful even. About a week passed before he noticed he wasn't feeling grateful anymore.

He hadn't thought of his son in a long time. Neglected memories reared up, reproachful, and for a moment he completely forgot about Raymond Sekowsky. By the time he looked back, Sekowsky had nearly reached his front door.

Right away Doug noticed something strange about the man's walk. The strange thing was how ordinary it was. There were no slumped shoulders; there was no sunken head. No solemn march or faltering step. Nothing like that. Doug didn't expect him to break down there in his front yard, but shouldn't his movements have offered a hint at least of his recent tragedy?

There even seemed to be, well maybe not quite a spring in his step, but yes, definitely a lightness, something loose-limbed and lively that animated his whole body as it carried him up the stairs to his door.

The next evening was the same, and the evening after. Between seven and seven thirty the Camry would pull into the driveway and Sekowsky would hop out, thrusting a jaunty elbow in front of the car door and slamming it shut with a twist from the waist. There would be the same incongruous walk to his door. Once he was inside, a pause, and then, behind a curtain, a single light would come on in what must have been the living room. (The other windows remained dark; there was never any sign of another Sekowsky.)

Doug had intended to come here and face the parents, to tell them who he was and, if he had the courage, to confess his crime. He'd felt a strange thrill at the thought of confession, a thrill that only grew stronger when the insurance agent warned him not to go. He had imagined the disconsolate parents: raw, hollow-eyed, their slack faces not sad so much as baffled, the faces of people who have closed themselves around a question they don't expect an answer to. Then he had seen Raymond Sekowsky walk to his front door. Doug tried not to hold that walk against him. People, he reminded himself, deal with tragedy in different ways, and a cheery bounce in his step did not preclude mourning going on inside where he couldn't observe it. But the more he watched that walk from car to front door, the more obscene it started to seem, an insult to the kid's memory, as if Sekowsky were coming home every evening to caper across his lawn in a shiny party hat.

And then there was his behavior at the shopping mall.

On Saturday afternoon Raymond Sekowsky left his house,

drove to the mall, and sat for a long time on a bench in front of the LensCrafters with a bag of Pretzel Time Cinnamon Sugar Bites. At first Doug took this as possible evidence of grief, since he just sat there all by himself with a peculiar strained look on his face. But then he noticed the Forever 21 next to the Lens-Crafters. When teenage girls entered or left Sekowsky's head would turn surreptitiously, his hand would freeze in the bag, and he would follow them with his eyes until they were out of sight. Then he would innocently resume munching until other teenage girls passed. Sometimes he leaned past the fern to get a longer look.

How would the kid—why did Doug resist using his name? To keep him at arm's length? To make him less specific and there-fore less human? Or was it that calling him by his name seemed presumptuous, as if he were pretending that he knew the kid, when in fact he didn't know him as anything other than a flash of moving color followed by a shape twitching on the street? Anyway, how would the kid feel if he were here to see that, instead of staying home and grieving and possibly drinking too much, his father was spending his Saturday afternoon eating Cinnamon Sugar Bites and leering at underage girls? But—Doug would have explained to the kid—this behavior could, if you thought about it, simply indicate a need to escape from his feelings. Lonely people often went to public places. Maybe he found solace in the parade of young lives marching past. Some of these girls must have been the kid's own age. Some of them might even have known him. Maybe Sekowsky was consid-ering this as he watched the girls. Or maybe he was imagining his son, alive, sitting there watching the girls in his place. The point was, Doug and the kid couldn't know with any certainty what was going through the father's mind. So what would have looked to the kid like leering if he were there, peeking from behind the wedding card rack of the Hallmark's with Doug, might not have been leering at all . . .

But there would have been no way to explain to the kid's satisfaction the incident the next afternoon. Sekowsky came out of his house with a bag of garden wood chips, walked onto his lawn, and started adding chips to the ones already there. Doug could see his lips puckering as he poured the chips from a hole in the bag's corner. His lips puckered, and even though Doug was too far away to hear, he knew, as the man scattered chips across the speckled, sunlit length of his garden, puckering and scattering and repuckering and sometimes squatting to smooth and sculpt the growing mounds, he knew that Raymond Sekowsky was whistling.

❀   ❀   ❀

Sekowsky left his house a little after noon. Doug watched him lock his front door, swing the keys around their ring with a flourish and drop them in his pocket.

Afterward, they claimed premeditation. A plan. It wasn't true, not in the sense that they meant it. If anything, it was because he couldn't decide what to do that he had come. He was hoping a confrontation might force some kind of decision out of him.

Later, he often regretted not being able to say he was drunk when it happened. It would have made everything easier to explain. But the fact was he had taken just one gulp from his flask, and that was more of a token confidence-builder than anything else. The blood alcohol content measured during the arrest—this time they actually gave him the Breathalyzer test—

was a result of all the drinking he did while he waited in the car for the police to arrive.

Doug had been about to get out of his car and go knock on the door when it opened and Sekowsky came out instead. So instead Doug sat, damp and jittery, hand on the car door latch, unable to persuade himself to move, while Sekowsky crossed the lawn and got into his own car.

Allowing himself one drink, he realized, had been a mistake. He should have allowed himself two, or three, or as many as it took to be able to do something he couldn't take back. He'd imagined himself getting out and confronting Raymond Sekowsky there at his front door. Confronting him with what? Insufficient mourning? No, not just that: with being a bad father. Yes, that was it: bad father. Angry words, back and forth. He would tackle Sekowsky. Sekowsky would tackle him. Either way, it wouldn't matter. A tussle there in the grass. One of them beaten bloody. But he had never been violent, drunk or otherwise. He didn't seem to have it in him.

So then why had he hit the gas pedal when the kid raced in front of him?

He kept asking himself this as Sekowsky pulled out of his driveway and drove down the street. He already knew where they were going. Sure enough, ten minutes later they turned into the mall's giant parking lot. The lot was divided into sections marked with animal signs, big colored signs on posts to help you remember where you'd parked your car. They were in the Giraffe section.

Sekowsky managed to find a space right away. Doug circled. There was no hurry. He had a pretty good idea where Sekowsky was going to end up: back on the bench in front of the Lens-Crafters, his hand in a bag of Cinnamon Sugar Bites. And Doug would end up in the Hallmark's again. He saw the scene as if he were spying on someone: a man stands at a wedding card rack, fraudulently fingering a lacy card while he peeks through the glass. He didn't recognize himself in that scene. That man wasn't him. It was clear enough what he should do: leave the parking lot and go home. But leaving felt like a surrender. Like giving up on ever figuring out what killing the kid had meant. He circled the Giraffe section, thinking he would park and thinking he would leave and doing neither.

Ahead, down near the end of the row, Raymond Sekowsky stepped out from behind a pickup.

He felt dizzy, as if the circles he'd been making in the car had been getting smaller and smaller. Then panic, and with it a hatred for himself more vivid than anything he'd ever felt before.

Raymond Sekowsky was walking, his back to Doug, in the direction of the mall. And his walk, as he went, was—what else?—buoyant and carefree.

Doug hit the gas and turned the steering wheel slightly, altering his trajectory.

In those few seconds before he changed his mind and slammed on the brakes, he understood something. He knew it as the car hurtled forward, his head tingling crazy warning: he had never done this before. This experience was new. He hadn't hit the kid on purpose after all. There was no time for him then to consider why he'd needed to blame himself, no time to locate and name the guilt he'd been secretly hoarding since long before the accident. He only knew this: he wasn't a killer. Foot on the pedal, he rushed toward a collision not yet too late to stop, paralyzed with disappointment and something like joy. He wasn't a killer. He was innocent.

The Visitors

When Dr. Tauber imagined the woman with the unpronounceable name, as he did more and more frequently, it was always without her son. In his daydreams, the boy was as absent as the husband. Only the woman was there, at his office, in his bedroom, on the stairs, clothed or unclothed, and although even in his fantasies he couldn't imagine her speaking his language, whatever he said to her she understood perfectly.

He didn't know what to call the distraction she'd become. What he felt for her, if it was love, what he felt for her was love, if it was. He trudged through a morning, labored across a dark afternoon. If it was love. He leaned into a face, conscious of tainted breath and the periapical swell of an acute abscess. He ate dinner from a plastic tray that nearly burned his fingers when he pulled it, unthinking, from the microwave.

Why the need to give the feeling a name? In the morning he waited for five minutes on the stairs, but she and her son didn't appear. Then the hated ascent to his office. Wasn't the feeling more genuine if it remained nameless? He traced gold inlay over the craze line of a maxillary premolar. But possibly that was the point: by naming it he might bracket it. Build a fence around it. The bright memory: her handing him a pair of onions.

He paused, sickle probe in hand, to look at them, oversized and lopsided on a silver tray, shadowed in an alcove like a shrine.

❀   ❀   ❀

"Are you okay?" the voice—a child's voice—had asked.

He was hunched over a handrail, taking his customary break in the morning climb up the hill. They had stopped four steps above. He noticed the woman first, face dark and steeply angled and creased diagonally along the forehead. Then the boy beside her, nine maybe or ten. Her jacket was too small for her and the boy's too large. That was one common characteristic of the Visitors: mismatched clothes, or improperly sized, or belonging to yesterday's fashion, a piecemeal assemblage of parts that gave them a scarecrowlike, patched-together look.

Was he okay: what a question. Did he *look* okay? He didn't say this but thought it. He didn't say this because he was in no condition to speak, occupied as he was with breathing and coughing and handrail-gripping to prevent a backward tumble down the hill. On the other hand, this was a fairly ordinary morning. This moment occurred every morning; it simply occurred at a progressively lower point on the stairs as the months and years and decades passed.

When he first set up his practice on the hill he'd told himself that the stairs would keep him young; when it was no longer possible to make that argument, he'd maintained that the stairs were, at least, preserving him; when what the stairs were doing, it had eventually become clear, was killing him. Slowly wearing down bone and joint and ligament and muscle. His ex-wife, who as his dental assistant had needed to brave the same stairs, had wanted to relocate. But their apartment, he'd reminded her—the apartment he now lived in alone—was a seven-minute walk away; they would never find a more convenient location. As much as he hated to admit it, she'd probably been right all along. Now, though, it was too late: if there had ever been a time when he might have summoned the resources to find a new office, to move equipment, to establish and groom new patients, that time was over. He would never know how many patients he had lost to the stairs; how many, especially the older ones who made up most of the neighborhood, had given up and gone somewhere less demanding. But there was one small advantage: the patients who did come arrived breathless and exhausted, and he'd always suspected that this made them more willing to sink gratefully into the dental chair and open their mouths to the needle and drill . . .

Of course Dr. Tauber also arrived breathless and exhausted. These days a minimum of thirty minutes was required before he felt capable of wielding needle or drill or any tool for that matter, which was why he arrived at the foot of the hill every morning at eight twenty. Occasionally people passed as he made his gradual way up the stairs, neighbors usually on their way to work, but he had never encountered Visitors here before.

They stood silently above him, watching him gasp and hack. The woman prodded the boy and he said it again—"Are you okay?"—in a tone that made the question sound like an accusation.

Dr. Tauber held up a hand: Wait.

So it was her question. Her concern.

"Thirty-two years here," he replied when he was eventually

capable of speech. "You'd think I'd be used to it." Smiling at the woman he realized she hadn't understood a word. She looked down at the boy.

"I've been here for thirty-two years now," he repeated slowly to the child, "and I'm still not used to these stairs. Do you understand?" The boy nodded. "Well tell her then." He drew an impatient line with his finger from the boy to the woman. "Tell her what I said."

The boy emitted an arrhythmic blurt of sound. When he'd finished, the woman turned to smile at Dr. Tauber, diagonal crease gone.

"So you live here on the hill?" Dr. Tauber asked, although he was fairly certain he already knew where they were living, where they *must* be living.

The boy nodded.

Looking at the mother so the boy would understand that Dr. Tauber was addressing her and that the boy was only required to translate, he said: "I guess that makes us neighbors. I have my office here, on the top of the hill. I'm Dr. Tauber, by the way. Edward. Call me Edward."

The boy blurted sounds; somewhere in the middle of it Dr. Tauber recognized his name. The woman put a hand to her chest and said something unidentifiable that he knew must be her own name. Indicating her son, she spoke again; this time he thought he detected a strangled "gaa" between clicked and throated consonants.

"Right!" he said. "Well, nice meeting you. Better get back to it. These stairs, you know!" And, nodding abruptly, he stepped past them, resuming his climb. He'd had a feeling, as she pronounced the unpronounceable names: a neighbor might be watching. From a window or doorway, from the top or possibly from the foot of the stairs, somewhere a gossipy neighbor, watching him chat with the Visitors.

They were called "the Visitors" in the neighborhood even though it had become clear that they were not visiting. That they were staying. Once the state revealed its plan to put on the hill, in the abandoned dormitory of the old polytechnic institute, these people fleeing from—was it conflict? drought? redrawn borders?—anyway some calamity or other, a petition had been circulated, led by an old woman named Marie. Dr. Tauber knew her as well as he knew anyone there, having for three decades attended the gradual disintegration of her teeth. Sweet and soft-spoken, with a lisp now due to her recently installed dental plate, she was not the obvious candidate to rally the residents against what she was calling "the Vithitorth." He hadn't wanted to sign the petition. Not due to any particular sympathy for "displaced persons," who—with the exception of the man that limped up the stairs every Monday to deliver dental supplies—seemed less like "persons" than statistical abstractions from a news report. His reluctance was due, rather, to a fundamental distrust of joining causes. Of joining any- thing, really: his ex-wife's most frequent complaint had been his supposed remoteness; the only time he ever let himself get close to people, she used to say, was when he was leaning over them in mask and gloves. His fear was that signing the petition might rope him into unforeseen responsibilities. But Marie's argument was sound: if these Visitors were allowed to come it might scare current residents away and discourage others from moving in, resulting in a loss of business for him. What she didn't say, what was not even hinted at by her but remained nevertheless firmly in his mind, was that refusing to participate might be seen as less than neighborly by his patients on the hill. So he had signed, his name added to a long list of mostly elderly residents, and there followed a festive adorning of the neighborhood in brightly colored posters, yard signs, and banners, and Dr. Tauber was surprised to see Marie's name in a newspaper article about the issue. A decision had been made, not an official announcement but a rumor interpreted as one: the dormitory would not be used after all. They had won. And although there was nothing that could be described as a celebration, there was a general sense of relief.

Then one evening, on his way home, he'd seen the gate to the dormitory open for the first time in years. He could hear hammering, pipes clanging. A few weeks later, other sounds could be heard beyond the gate. The sounds of children: shouts and cries and laughter reaching him on the stairs together with the smell of unfamiliar food cooking. And nearly overnight the hill had become noisier, wilder, infused with a volatile new life . . .

There were no further petitions. Now that the Visitors were there, the residents didn't have the heart, it seemed, or at any rate the bad manners, to demand their removal. There were children after all, mothers and children . . .

The particular mother and child that Dr. Tauber had met on the stairs became a common sight as he made his morning climb. The boy, he learned, had just started attending the local grade school. Dr. Tauber got the impression that it might have been his first time attending school in America, but he didn't dare ask where the boy had learned English, just as he didn't ask where they'd been living or what they'd been doing before coming to the hill. When he spoke with them—or rather with the mother by means of the boy's sullen translation—he made a point of avoiding tactless questions about their previous lives. He told her once about a nearby park with a playground. Another time he recommended one supermarket over another. There were mornings when they didn't appear, and mornings when he found himself disappointed to see her going down the stairs with other mothers and children; and on those mornings it was astonishing to see her speaking in her language, voluble and animated, with a boisterous laugh he wouldn't have expected from her. She was like a different person, and he realized how much the constraints of translation must be stifling her when they talked. Embarrassed, he tried to ignore her then, but she always smiled and waved, even when the other mothers glared at him stone-faced.

In their encounters she never used English, although she must have learned enough to offer a simple greeting at least, a "hello" or "how are you." At times it seemed she understood more than she let on; at other times he was convinced she understood nothing at all . . . The boy's English, on the other hand, continued to improve as the months passed, until he sounded like any American child. His interpreting skills, however, remained as poor as ever. It wasn't just his sparse vocabulary; it was, more than anything else, his attitude: he regarded Dr. Tauber with unconcealed suspicion, and provided only the barest translation in either direction. Dr. Tauber would see layers of feeling cross the woman's features as she spoke, only to hear the boy deliver in his terse monotone a phrase about seasonal fruit or the unreliability of the local buses. It was as if he were trying to flatten the contents he was transmitting to a single dimension, extracting any depth or substance. Sometimes Dr. Tauber felt that the boy was more of a barrier than a bridge. It might be better, he thought, if the son weren't there at all; then he and the woman could communicate unimpeded, learning to read each other in a pure, wordless language of gestures and facial expressions . . .

The boy seemed to wish he didn't need to be there either. He perked up only once, when Dr. Tauber complained about the snowfall that had made the stairs even more treacherous than usual.

"I like it," the boy said, suddenly defiant. "I like *snow*." Placing on the word a grave emphasis that was apparently the closest he came to ordinary childlike enthusiasm.

"He likes snow?" Dr. Tauber grinned at the woman. "With these stairs?"

The boy grunted affirmation.

"No, no. It's for her. That was for your mother." With his finger Dr. Tauber made the invisible-line gesture from boy to woman that meant a translation was required.

After the boy finished the woman spoke. "We don't have snow," the boy explained. "At home."

"At home? . . . Ah, right. Well of course: no snow." He tried to imagine it: all heat and light and crumbling surfaces the color of dust. "That must be . . ." He stopped; he'd nearly ventured into a region he had no wish to explore.

"I have one of my own," he said to the woman instead. "A son. Much older now of course. When he was your son's age he loved the snow too. Couldn't get enough of it." Dr. Tauber waited for the translation, then continued: "We used to build snowmen." He turned to the boy. "Have you made one yet?" He wanted her to see that he was good with children. That he could be kind to her son.

The boy looked at Dr. Tauber as if he didn't understand English any better than his mother.

". . . A snowman," Dr. Tauber said. "A man made out of snow.

Sticks, a carrot. Maybe a hat, like Frosty. Frosty? You don't . . . You must have seen one." Squatting, he formed a small mound of dirty snow on the step above, squeezed together a slushball and set it on top.

Mother and son looked down at what he'd made.

He stood up. "Well this isn't much of an example." His shoe toppled it, crushed the shape flat. "Sometime we'll have to . . ." He was about to say "build one together." But something about the boy prevented him from behaving, even for a moment, in a fatherly way . . .

And the boy's actual father? Gone, Dr. Tauber was sure. Left behind in their sunbright, snowless country. Lost. Killed, possibly, in a war. Anyway permanently absent from the woman's story . . .

He arrived at the stairs at eight fifteen now so he wouldn't miss her if she left early. He would wait in the cold on his usual step even after he'd finished catching his breath. And it began to seem to him that the moment when she appeared at the dormitory gate and descended to him, that this moment and not the office one hundred and thirty-three steps above was the reason he was on the stairs at all. Or that in any case it was this moment that allowed him to survive the superficial variety and underlying sameness of his days. Often they only exchanged pleasantries or smiled at each other as they passed, but he felt nevertheless as if he were receiving a day's worth of some essential sustenance, enough—if only barely—to carry him through the long hours above spent presiding over ruin and decay . . .

He'd never needed this sustenance before. Or: he'd needed it and hadn't known it. He'd gotten something once from dentistry, not sustenance perhaps, but a craftsman's pleasure at least, professional curiosity when a mouth opened and accomplishment when it closed and the Dixie cup filled with water . . . In the beginning of his career, when he was just out of dental school, a mouth had been a landscape. Mountains, cliffs, caverns: and the mouth itself a cavern. Caves within dank caves. What a mystery a mouth was! The secrets people held behind their lips. His first year in private practice: that elegant lady with the fanglike cuspid snaggletoothed in her upper left quadrant. Nothing could have been more charming. When she opened her mouth to him, he wanted to profess his adoration then and there. It wasn't even sexual, or yes, possibly it was, but not in the obvious sense; it was the shy and reluctant revelation of a flaw. An opened mouth was a confession. He never looked into their eyes. It felt invasive. Too much. They were already vulnerable; he was already the master even as he was a supplicant before them. They lay frozen in the ergonomic chair, helpless, beyond humiliation. In surgery at least the patient was anesthetized; the conquest was hidden from the conquered. Here they opened themselves voluntarily, they chose to surrender to him . . .

When had this surrender stopped feeling like a privilege? It wasn't that the woman had replaced the pleasure of dentistry; her presence simply reminded him that he must have lost it at some point long before, and that he'd been existing since with nothing to put in its place. Still, his work, and his devotion to it, had continued to provide something. Balance and order, for example. His life hadn't been unbearable; if there was loneliness and an absence of joy, he'd barely noticed. And meeting her had brought . . . what? Imbalance; disorder. An incursion of the unknown into what had until then seemed a perfectly satisfactory existence. It was clear what he'd lost; but what had he gained? Momentary and meaningless encounters on the stairs with a woman who didn't even speak his language.

He'd decided to stop waiting for her there, and was even considering going to work earlier or later to avoid seeing her, when, one morning, the woman reached into her shoulder bag and produced a pair of giant onions.

She held them up, one in each hand.

"Onions," Dr. Tauber said. *"Un-yunz."* Enunciating carefully, thinking she might be asking for the English name.

She took a step closer, stretched her arms toward him.

"For me?" Dr. Tauber glanced at the boy. His face, as usual, was giving up nothing. And the woman's face? He'd hoped he could learn to decipher it; but he couldn't have named what he saw there as she set the onions on his palms.

"Ah. Really? You shouldn't . . . That's, well, thank you." She shook her head and, smiling, said something, but the boy provided no translation. Then they left, Dr. Tauber still holding up the onions as if on display, feeling somehow it was wrong to lower his hands.

He didn't eat the onions; instead he placed them on a stainless dental tool tray and set the tray in an alcove beside his desk. He didn't know what to make of it. Was it a custom in her country to give onions to neighbors? Or her own odd but endearing idiosyncrasy? Or was it, conceivably, something else—some kind of sign? He was afraid to read too much into it. Nevertheless, it wasn't completely implausible that the gift contained a meaning he was meant to understand. He might not have been as young as her, but he was distinguished and he was a doctor and in her country the idea of a younger woman and a man not yet old but somewhat older might be perfectly acceptable or even preferable since the mature man, if a professional like himself, would be in a position to take care of— But he was getting ahead of himself . . .

What he felt for her: it wasn't as though it represented a return to the lost feelings of his youth. He couldn't remember ever feeling this for his wife, or for either of the women he'd dated in dental school. But maybe all of this—the sad and persistent yearning, the daydreams, the unmoored helplessness he experienced when he looked at a pair of onions on a tool tray—maybe it was all a symptom of something other than *love*, whatever that word might want to mean. An unusually concentrated form of gratitude, for instance. How often was he given vegetables? How often was he given anything? And if not precisely gratitude, an emotion perhaps without a proper name in his language, and impossible therefore to convey to her. But actions, he reminded himself, speak louder than words: what, after all, was her gift if not a wordless action? He could repay her, and show his feelings (whatever they were), with the action he performed best . . . Then again, no: offering to examine her mouth at no charge might be taken the wrong way . . .

"Thank you again for the onions," he said the next time they met. "They were delicious. And I wanted to show my appreciation."

He waited for the translation. With an open hand the woman made a sign of erasure. He ignored it and forged on: "I don't know if I mentioned it, but I'm a dentist actually." When the boy hesitated, he clarified: "I'm a . . . tooth doctor. I fix teeth." Baring his own, he tapped his incisors with a forefinger.

He had to use the finger to make the invisible-line gesture before the boy reluctantly translated.

"And your son," he said, "I was thinking I'd be happy, you know, to give him an oral diagnosis. A dental checkup. *Pro bono publico*, as they say. Free of charge. Just my way of . . .

Just. Well." He smiled down at the boy. "Go ahead, tell her. Tell her I can check your teeth for you."

For a moment the boy stared silently back at him. Then, without taking his eyes off Dr. Tauber, he said something to his mother.

She reacted not with words or a change in expression but bodily, lurching backward like she'd been pushed and nearly tripping on the step behind her. She recovered her balance and took the boy's arm. And then they were passing him, two dwindling figures descending the stairs and vanishing around a corner.

He stood holding the handrail, waiting as if—although he knew better—they might reappear at any moment.

He spent the weekend reenacting the scene in his mind. What had he done? Did the offer of dental care in her culture constitute some unforgivable faux pas? Maybe it was rude to have used the words *pro bono*, as if they were indigents unable to pay. Or did she simply dislike dentists? By Monday he'd half convinced himself that her reaction had nothing to do with him or what he'd said. There were any number of possibilities, he thought, arriving even earlier than usual to wait for them. But the way she gripped her son's hand as they came down the stairs—and on the other side of the handrail!—without once looking in his direction had already confirmed the worst even before she ignored the "Good morning!" he called out in the most ordinary tone he could muster.

That afternoon, after the limping man had completed his delivery of dental supplies, Dr. Tauber stopped him outside his office.

"Excuse me."

He closed the door so Angela, his receptionist and dental assistant, wouldn't hear.

"A question. If you don't mind. In your country people receive dental care, yes? I mean, of course you do. And it's not common to . . . You *are* from the same country, am I right? As the Vis—as the people in the old dormitory down the hill?"

Was *country* the proper word? It might be a region. Or something else: a borderless wasteland; a land with new and arbitrary borders . . .

Yes," the man said. Then added (proudly? contemptuously?), "But I don't know those people."

"Well of course not. It's not like I think you all . . . Of course not. It's just that I need to . . . clear something up."

There had been a slight misunderstanding, Dr. Tauber explained, during a discussion about an appointment. He left out the onions and the offer of free dental care. Nothing in the man's manner indicated a willingness to help or even any interest in the matter—he seemed, if anything, impatient to return to his deliveries—but Dr. Tauber was nevertheless able to recruit him to act, however reluctantly, as translator.

At the dormitory gate Dr. Tauber hesitated for an instant, feeling suddenly like a trespasser. The building, salmon-colored stucco, looked more like a motel than a dormitory: three stories of doors behind rusted walkways faced a treeless courtyard of weeds and shattered concrete. He realized he had no real information to give the man: he didn't know their apartment number; the woman's name he couldn't possibly repeat; the only thing he remembered about the boy's name was that strangled "gaa" . . . The most he could provide was a brief physical description of the two.

The man hobbled over to a little girl kicking a ball against the building. She pointed at a door on the second floor. They climbed iron stairs. As the man knocked, Dr. Tauber halted behind him and then took three steps back. He was no longer convinced of the husband's permanent absence. He might be there, on the other side of the door: hairy and brutish and nearly bursting out of mismatched clothes . . .

When the door opened, though, it was a woman. Another woman. He'd assumed finding her would be straightforward: how many families could there be with a single mother (if she was a single mother) and a boy of his age? Five, as it turned out. When they left, the woman kept her door open in spite of the chill, peering out at them as they went down the hall. The same thing happened at the next door they tried: a knock; the wrong woman; a face peering out as they left. All around him, he could sense them—a woman with a laundry basket; a pair of teenage boys—stopping in their tracks to watch him. Even the little girl: ball abandoned, she stood on the cracked concrete observing Dr. Tauber and the limping man as they went back and forth, from floor to floor, conducting their search. Maybe they thought he was there in some official capacity, to inspect or investigate or deport. But he didn't feel empowered by the attention. He felt, instead, furtive and self-conscious, as though he were the Visitor, wandering an unknown land without a proper visa . . .

Finally a door opened—number 7, first floor—and this time it was her. Dr. Tauber stayed back, in the courtyard, wishing there was a tree he could hide behind. But then she spotted him, and he regretted standing so far away: it made him look like some suspect character lurking in the distance. The limping man spoke. And then they were exchanging those sounds of theirs, at first tentatively, then with increasing urgency from her and lengthening stretches of silence from him, until she said one last thing and closed the door.

The man swung around, and for a second Dr. Tauber thought he was about to get hit.

"You are a shame," the man hissed.

"I'm a what?"

The man lurched past Dr. Tauber, then stopped.

"Here, you people. You think about you only. What you want, you say. But what you said to her? In my country, you can't say such things."

"Can't say . . . what? Dentists can't offer free dental care?"

"Can't . . . I don't know the word. A shame. To want to be . . . not her husband. To be like her husband. To want to . . ."

"What? But that's ridiculous. I never . . . I never said anything of the kind!"

The man looked skeptical. More than skeptical.

"No: listen to me. I'm telling you, I never said anything like— There was a mistake. A mistake in the translation. Must have been. I used the words *pro bono*. It's Latin. It means 'for the common good.' In other words no charge. I offered to examine her son's teeth at no charge. Nothing else. Maybe the boy misheard me. Or didn't understand."

Although the man didn't appear completely convinced, he was eventually persuaded to return to her door, where he knocked, repeating something in his language, until it opened. Dr. Tauber wasn't sure if it was safe to move closer but he did, until he was almost at the door himself. The woman's face was set and hard; the diagonal crease he'd seen that first time had returned. The man gestured toward Dr. Tauber as he spoke.

"I'm not a bad man!" Dr. Tauber interrupted, afraid that before the man could finish the door might close forever. "Tell her! No: don't tell her that. Tell her my intentions are not . . .

My intentions are to help her. To help her son. To check his teeth. She gave me onions."

The man translated.

As she listened, the woman's face lost its hard focus, then went slack and inward with some kind of understanding. And Dr. Tauber, succeeding finally in reading her face, understood as well: he knew what had happened.

Leaving the door half open, she disappeared inside. When she returned, her son was beside her. They stood formally in the doorway until she touched the back of the boy's head.

"Sorry," he murmured, wet eyes glistening with hatred.

She touched his head again (but tenderly; why so tenderly?).

"I'm sorry," he said, louder this time. "For lying."

The woman spoke.

"She says her son has afraid of dentists," the man told him.

"Right. Well." Dr. Tauber cast an amiable expression in the boy's general direction, avoiding his eyes. "It wouldn't be the first time. Children and dentists. Anyway, no harm done. Water under the bridge. It's an expression. All is forgiven, basically."

He waited for the man to translate and then continued: "The main thing is that I'm here to help. I want your son to learn he has nothing to be afraid of."

❂   ❂   ❂

Ordinarily Dr. Tauber didn't work on weekends, but he made an exception, arranging the appointment for three o'clock on a Saturday afternoon—there was no need, after all, to involve Angela in this informal *pro bono* case, with its unclear issues regarding the necessity of legal forms and insurance, among other things. He'd put on lab coat and gloves and set a mask under his chin, and was anxious to see the woman's reaction to the sight of him in uniform, but when they arrived at the reception area she gazed past him, at the scene framed in the window: rooftops and miniature trees and a skyline of distant buildings glittering in the sun.

She put her fingertips to the glass and exhaled a sound or a word.

"Quite a view, isn't it?" he said, making a grand gesture that encompassed the entire city, as if in the sweep of his arm he was offering it all to her.

The boy wasn't looking out the window. He was staring through the doorway at the still-darkened operatory.

"Ready to get started?" Dr. Tauber walked over to him. "Follow me."

The woman was about to go with them, but he barred her way with a smile and pointed toward the reception area's sofa and magazine rack. As much as he wanted her near him, he needed the boy alone so he would understand the hopelessness of his situation; the fact that there would be no rescue.

He turned on the lights and guided the boy inside. The boy made it to the middle of the room before coming to a stop. He seemed a genuine child for the first time, frozen in place beside Dr. Tauber and giving off something as vital and primitive as an odor . . .

He saw through the boy's eyes all of the room's familiar objects: the aseptic gleam of the arrayed instruments; the curved chair waiting to contain; and looming above it the operatory light that a girl had once told him looked like an insect's head. And in a moment, once he'd adjusted the mask over his face and the dental loupes over his eyes, Dr. Tauber would loom over the boy as well like something other than himself . . .

Once a child had seen all of that: there was usually no way
to bribe or persuade or trick a mouth into opening then. And
he never tried. He may not have been a pediatric dentist—as
the neighborhood aged, he had, if anything, by default come
to specialize in geriodontics—but he had, over the years, dealt
with more than his share of uncooperative children. And he
ordinarily favored a no-nonsense approach. He decided, however, that in this case he would not, under any circumstances,
use a bite block: he would rather risk a bitten finger than lock
the boy's mouth in place. He wanted the boy's consent; he
wanted the boy to submit willingly.

He was curt and a bit stern without being too forbidding.
Sit here. Head back. Relax. I'm going to adjust the chair now.
No, hold still, it's just a bib. The boy's reactions were slow, dis-
turbingly delayed. He didn't cringe or scream or struggle the
way some children did, but Dr. Tauber sensed the clamped jaw.
The coiled resistance. Panic had clouded over all of the intelli-
gence in the boy's eyes. Relax, Dr. Tauber commanded. Which
meant: Give up. Yield. He put a thumb to the boy's chin and
said, Open. And when the boy did finally yield and the lips
parted, it was like a magical transformation from animal into
compliant human, and Dr. Tauber felt triumphant and heart-
broken. After that it was praise that worked, simple praise and
he was no longer stern but cheerful and avuncular.

The teeth were perfect. There were no fractures; no biofilm
deposits; no malocclusions. Permanent dentition was developing normally, with no over-retention among the primary
teeth. No sign of gingival inflammation. Not a single carious
lesion. A complete absence of expected hypodontia or micro-
dontia: each neat row was uniform and complete. Who could
say when the boy had last received care? Who could say if he'd

ever received care? And here it was, a miracle: a pristine mouth, immaculate, uncorrupted.

When the boy had rinsed and the bib had been removed, Dr. Tauber took off his mask and loupes, helped the child down off the dental chair, and led him back to the reception area.

"It's not good news, I'm afraid," he said to the woman. "There's a lot of work to be done." He waited for her son to speak, knowing the boy could be trusted now to translate correctly, then continued: "More visits will be required. Quite a few. At no charge, of course. Don't worry though: it's not a hopeless case. I've seen worse. With the right care, his teeth can be saved. I'm going to help your son."

He was already devising a course of action. The miracle of the perfect mouth would be maintained. For the next appointment: radiographic examination followed by routine cleaning, fluoride treatment, and instruction in oral hygiene. Then regular preventive visits to monitor incipient decay and the exfoliation of the remaining primary teeth. And in several years, with the onset of adolescence, the potential for new and interesting problems: ankylosis; ectopic eruption; the need for orthodontic care. Yes: there was a lot of work to be done. Many visits that, over the course of time, might prove necessary for the patient; many explanatory consultations with the parent . . .

The dark oval of her face swam suddenly near. She was moving toward him. Reaching out to take his still-gloved hand with both of hers. She spoke. He didn't need a translation to know that she was thanking him. He let her grip his hand. His own grip, he felt sure, was professionally firm and neutral. Whatever was trembling inside him didn't reach his fingers. He'd always been proud of this ability to separate heart from hands. With age some men lost the steady touch. And Dr. Tauber had himself been younger, there was no denying it, he'd been younger and would never be as young again as at this moment, with her close, gripping him through his glove, speaking words to him he seemed almost to understand. But the hands were as solid as ever: none of the shaking that spelled the end of a career in dentistry.

Winter Crane

As you approach the mountain resort of Tateshina—after the final twist in the road, and just before the sudden dip that gives you your first view of the town, barnacled around the lake rim in white-gray clusters far below—you will see, on your right, a billboard welcoming you to "the home of the Silver-Crested Winter Crane, our own Loch Ness Monster!" Beside these words the bird is painted in mid-flap, beak pointing skyward, wing tips extending beyond the sign's borders, a nice touch that, for just a second, as the sign comes into view, creates the illusion of three-dimensionality, of motion even, as if the bird is leaving the flat confines of the board for the actual unpainted sky.

❀   ❀   ❀

Until recently, the earliest surviving pictorial representation of the Winter Crane was believed to be an Edo-period sliding-door panel attributed to Kano Tan'yu (1602–1674). The painting, ink and color on paper, shows the bird in the foreground, legs buried in snow. Snow—depicted negatively through the simple use of blank space—surrounds the crane, filling most of the panel. It is a spare, austere painting, and has for this reason been associated with Kano's later screen work; aside from the bird itself, the only colors are a small patch of green in the lower left corner, where snow has melted, and, to the right of the crane, a single cherry blossom petal drifting above its blue shadow. The petal suggests a sudden spring snow. Wings partly unfolded, the bird has lifted its head and opened its red beak as if to sing or to cry out. The pose is dynamic and evocative; what exactly it evokes, though, is open to dispute: it has been variously interpreted as celebrating the arrival of spring and mourning the end of winter.

For many years the screen resided in the home of a private collector in Austria, having arrived there under somewhat shadowy circumstances. When it was put up for auction in 1998, experts examining the piece claimed it to be a forgery, created in the twentieth century. Does the original screen reside somewhere else? Was it destroyed at some point in the past? Or was the *Winter Crane* never in fact the work of Kano Tan'yu at all, but rather a fabrication, a myth, the creation of the forger?

❊   ❊   ❊

The billboard's comparison of the bird to the Loch Ness Monster is no doubt confusing to the average tourist, coming in winter for the skiing or in summer to escape the humidity of the lower altitudes. These people know the crane, if at all, from the common folktale describing its origin; the only flying creatures they hope to see in Tateshina are the famous hang-gliders who wheel above the town in their polyester wings. Even to those arriving on tour buses for the express purpose of spotting the bird, the hyperbole of the sign may be hard to fathom. The Silver-Crested Winter Crane is, after all, not exactly a prehistoric monster. It is, however, in its own way perhaps no less elusive than "Nessie": although *Grus hiberna* has appeared in countless paintings and texts, and although there are many who claim to have seen it, the bird has to date never been captured or reliably photographed. You won't find it caged in any zoo or stuffed behind glass in any natural history museum. Officially listed as Highly Endangered, some ornithologists believe it is already extinct. And there are even those who argue that the Silver-Crested Winter Crane never existed at all, that its frequent appearance in Japanese works of art has always been as emblematic as the appearance in other cultures of unicorns or griffins.

Tateshina's claim on the crane is not due to actual sightings, but to the largely unsupported assertion that the folktale originated here before spreading throughout Japan. One thing is certain: the town has succeeded in promoting and capitalizing on the bird more successfully than any potential rivals in the region. Ornithologists devoted to preserving the crane complain that this commercialization only damages their cause, encouraging the notion that the threatened bird is fictitious, and reducing the chance that its plight will be taken seriously. Tateshina persists, though: every day tour buses drive past the billboard and descend to the town, carrying passengers eager for a glimpse of the legendary creature.

❁   ❁   ❁

And it turns out your love
Was about as real as a Winter Crane
—chorus to "Winter Crane," by Japanese
salsa/speedcore band The Clicking Mandibles
(translated from the Japanese)

❀   ❀   ❀

If the Winter Crane exists, it will not, most scientists believe, be found in Tateshina, or for that matter anywhere on Honshu, where agricultural development has resulted in severe habitat loss, but rather on the chain of uninhabited islands that speckle the Japan Sea. Uninhabited doesn't necessarily mean untouched, as regularly scheduled boats take ecotourists to the islands in search of the Winter Crane and other rare animals. These are day trips; Japanese law prohibits the public from camping or remaining overnight. The only exception made is for the Japanese Ornithological Society, which has established permanent research centers on a number of the islands. Most of the researchers are Japanese, but among them is a single American, ornithologist Richard Bedrosian. He is fluent in Japanese and seems at home there with his colleagues. Bedrosian originally came on a grant from the National Audubon Society to make a comparative study of the American Whooping Crane (*Grus Americana*) and the Japanese Red-Crowned Crane (*Grus japonensis*). While there he learned of the search for the controversial Silver-Crested Winter Crane. He has been visiting annually ever since.

Bedrosian is confident that the bird will be found. "There's no shortage of anecdotal evidence," he says. "Plenty of sightings. Then there's the secondary evidence—droppings and feathers, for example—that we feel fairly sure can be traced to the crane. It's only a matter of time before we come across a bird or a nest."

❀   ❀   ❀

What is the call of the Winter Crane? Does it resemble the brassy declaration of *Grus americana*? Or is it, like the call of its presumed cousin, *Grus japonensis*, a tremulous woodwind arpeggio, a three-note query? Or something else altogether? There is, surprisingly, no mention of it in the literature, with the exception of the origin myth, where it is simply called "sad." The crane has been painted, sculpted, described in great detail. We could draw it down to the last feather, but we have yet to hear its voice.

❊   ❊   ❊

The target demographic for Tateshina's Winter Crane tour is Japanese, elderly, and middle-class; more specifically, active seniors with an interest in Japanese history and legend. The tourists are transported in tall luxury buses equipped with tinted UV-blocking windows, vibrating massage seats, and pretty, white-gloved tour guides wearing three-pointed caps and smart epauletted uniforms that make them look like anime Intergalactic Space Fleet Officers. (By contrast, the budget tours aimed at younger consumers tend to be strictly no-frills, usually packed overnight buses bound for Tokyo Disneyland, Universal Studios Japan, or one of the meticulously replicated European villages—complete with imported foreigners in period dress—that can be found scattered in unlikely spots across the Japanese countryside.)

The tour, known as the "Winter Crane hike," is part of a larger package with a variety of options, all presented attractively in photo-illustrated brochures. In addition to visiting Tateshina, tourists can, for instance, fill plastic bottles with the restorative spring water trickling down a mossy fissure in a roadside cliff, the water blessed by the statue of the goddess Kannon a hundred meters above; visit the reconstructed site of the ancient Princess Himiko's palace; move in hooded raincoats through the dripping caves of Yamaguchi, where blind albino creatures swim in underwater streams; or photograph each other at the Sacred Temple of Seikenji, reputed scene of the monk-scholar Nenjin's self-immolation (which, grand name notwithstanding, turns out to be nothing more than a broken stone altar encircled by vending machines and a rusted link fence).

Arriving in Tateshina, the seniors descend and disembark, one after the other. The tour guide will already have stepped off the bus, and waits on the asphalt, smiling, a color-coded pennant on a stick held aloft so no one will get lost or end up following one of the other tours. But these are not doddering old fools. These seniors are, for the most part, alert and purposeful, cameras and binoculars ready. They follow the tour guide in their floppy hats and hiking boots, sturdy, genderless, leather-skinned, zippered pouches bulging from waists, like a special race evolutionarily adapted to the task of stalking the Winter Crane.

The tour guide ushers them across the parking lot, past the souvenir shops and breaded octopus stands—on the way back they will be given exactly ten minutes to make purchases—and then, lowering her pennant so it won't hit the branches, leads the way into the forest's maze of crisscrossing footpaths.

❀   ❀   ❀

The Origin of the Winter Crane

The Queen of the Moon had everything she might want in her kingdom of ice and snow—everything except for fish. She looked down on Man as he caught and cooked them, and the smell of the fish broiling in salt and bean oil rose up to her kingdom, filling her with envy. So she asked the River God to let her have a fish for her frozen waters, but the God refused. Incensed, the Queen waited until the full moon, when the wind blows the lunar drifts into a circle and the moonlight unfolds its broad path to the world, and then climbed down to a riverbank. As she caught a trout in her trap the River God, who had been secretly watching, rose up in a mighty splash and punished her by changing her into a crane. Her white skin grew into feathers, the rings on her fingers became silvery wing tips, and her crown was transformed into a silver crest.

"Now you can eat all the trout you like!" he said.

The Queen begged his forgiveness, stretching her long neck pitifully and flapping her beautiful wings until the God, relenting, said: "You may resume your true form—but only when your kingdom's light fills the sky; and you may return home—but for only one night each month, when the moon is full." By day she was condemned to live as a crane, remaining near the river and feeding on its creatures so she would forever be reminded of her misdeed. (In truth, the River God had fallen in love with the Queen, and wanted her bound to his side.)

❀   ❀   ❀

"I guess you could call it an obsession," Bedrosian admits with a laugh. "But it's not your typical . . . It's an obsession that sneaks up on you."

❀   ❀   ❀

At one time the Winter Crane was a common heraldic symbol. Most famously, it appeared on the coat of arms of feudal baron Hirai Masaie. Blamed for an assassination attempt on the life of regent Toyotomi no Hideyoshi, Masaie was forced to commit ritual suicide, his family was disgraced, and the Winter Crane abruptly vanished from heraldry, the regent having banned its use as a family crest. The crane, it was claimed, had been the identifying mark of the secret society formed by Masaie to topple the government. For years afterward, the Crane Society was rumored to persist, an invisible league of conspirators patiently plotting its coup against the regency. The bird had become synonymous with shame, treachery, and official paranoia. The symbol was later "rehabilitated" under the Tokugawa shogunate, and even underwent a brief vogue: flaunted as a sign of the new shogun's victory over the former regime, the crane gleamed atop official roofs, and shone silver and white across the gold foil of court panels. But the damage was done: the bird had been darkened in the public mind by mystery and intrigue, and even today this most Japanese of symbols is absent from the crests of virtually all Japanese families.

❀   ❀   ❀

And so the Queen wandered the world's rivers and streams. One morning, while chasing a frog through tall reeds, she found herself caught in a snare. When the trapper who had laid this snare came to check on it, he was surprised to see a strange bird thrashing its long wings and snapping desperately at its roped leg until its beak was red with blood. (This is the reason why the Winter Crane has a red beak.) The trapper watched, and experienced an unfamiliar feeling: part pity, and part exultation at the sight of beauty trapped there by his own crafty hand. And in gratitude for this new feeling that he couldn't name or understand, he let the bird go. It hopped away, graceless in its sudden freedom, then seemed to remember itself and took to the air. A hand shielding his eyes, the trapper stood there following its flight, turning slowly in place as the bird turned in the sky.

The Queen tried to leave the place, fearing the traps that the man cared for so lovingly, coiled and sleepless things that waited in shadows, patient as snakes. But she found herself returning, watching from above as the man collected his daily catch and took it home to the hut where he lived alone on the forest edge. And she found that she couldn't leave him, as if she were still caught in the snare and beating her white wings into the dirt.

So when night fell and moonlight returned her to her true form, she approached his hut in what she told herself must be gratitude for having been freed. The hut was empty; the man was still out trapping in the woods. The Queen entered to wait for him. When he finally returned, he stood gaping at her in the open doorway, his catch squirming in the bag dangling from his hand.

She told him she was lost and hungry. Once the trapper recovered, he offered to let her share his dinner. They ate pheasant and chestnuts and yams, new tastes that she relished. She devoured her food, ignoring his questions and forgetting, for the moment, her reason for coming. He gave up finally on trying to learn how this strange, pale woman had arrived at his hut. He told her she could remain for the night. When he woke at daybreak, she was gone. The next night she came again; and the next. But each morning he woke alone. The trapper, who had fallen in love with the Queen, begged her one night to live with him as his wife. She agreed, but made him promise two things: first, that he would never ask her where she went during the day or when the moon was full; and, second, that he would never try to follow her.

❀   ❀   ❀

For a long time those interested in the Silver-Crested Winter Crane had a hard time finding a home online. They were ridiculed when they ventured onto the terrain of serious bird-watchers, many of whom believe the crane to be apocryphal or extinct. Yet they found themselves equally unwelcome at cryptozoological forums devoted to Sasquatch, Bearwolves, and the fanged Puerto Rican goat-mutilating Chupacabra; the crane was perhaps too innocuous—it lacked glamour. So other sites developed, first in Japanese, but increasingly in other languages as well, featuring cell phone photos or video clips of blurred white birds in motion. Eventually clear pictures were posted too, lauded by some as proof of the bird's existence, derided by others as the result of clever photoshop editing. Online, the bird has flourished. The internet reports proliferate, as if the crane is reproducing, thriving in its new habitat, moving through blogs and jpegs and chat rooms in as yet mysterious migratory patterns . . .

❀   ❀   ❀

The Queen and the trapper lived happily together for many years until, one day, the trapper spotted a familiar bird drinking at a stream. He hid behind a tree and watched it, remembering the bird he had set free once, and remembering his nameless emotion at seeing the snared creature beat its wings and snap its bloody beak. And then he found himself thinking of his wife. Not as she was now, but as she had been when he opened the door of his hut and discovered her sitting there at his table, trembling slightly, watching him with terrified eyes and a smile like a grimace. She had reminded him of a wounded animal that had lost its senses and seemed ready to fly straight into the jaws of its pursuer.

The trapper followed the crane down the stream, moving silently from tree to tree, and as the evening waned and the light failed, he was shocked to see the bird making its way along the path to his hut. It opened the latch with its beak and stepped through the doorway. But when the trapper followed it inside, he found only his wife, waiting for him as always.

(All of this had been planned by the River God. Jealous of the love between the trapper and the Queen of the Moon, he had lured her with fast-moving trout to a point in the stream near where the man was setting his trap.)

The man said nothing to his wife, but he could not rid himself of a strange suspicion. Finally he was unable to resist: before dawn, when his wife rose as she always did and left the hut, he followed her into the woods, moving as stealthily as if he were hunting a wild animal. But the Queen sensed him behind her and, circling back, surprised him just as dawn broke. She opened her mouth to speak, perhaps to curse him for his betrayal, perhaps to forgive him for it, perhaps to say farewell. But before she could speak her red lips lengthened into a beak and her voice became a bird's sad call. Then she hopped out of reach and flew into the brightening sky.

She didn't return that night, or the next. And although the

trapper searched for her by day, and waited for her in his hut at night for weeks, then months, then years, she never returned.

❖   ❖   ❖

The common Japanese crane is often called "the bird of happiness." Sighting it is supposed to bring good luck. What, then, is the Winter Crane? What does sighting it bring?

❖   ❖   ❖

Bedrosian packs his things. First thaw will come soon. He'll be back next year, he says. He doesn't see the trip as a failure. He feels—although he realizes it's illogical—that each time he fails to locate the bird it brings him closer, as if each search is blacking out another section on a map until, finally, only one bright square will remain, and in the center of it a Silver-Crested Winter Crane, waiting.

❖   ❖   ❖

Midway between the cities of Fukuoka and Kitakyushu, next to the elevated highway, there is a love hotel called The Winter Crane. To be visible to drivers, the seven-story hotel has added a three-story façade which rises high enough so that the white neon characters for "Winter Crane," two stories high themselves, appear at eye level as you course along the highway. Passing the luminous white words, you experience—if you are among those who have found themselves becoming obsessed with the bird—a little jolt, as if the car has suddenly accelerated, even as you laugh at yourself for imagining, if for only a second, that a love hotel might offer some clue to the existence of the crane.

The hotel lobby presents straight-faced its chipped and faded burlesque of opulence: plaster statuettes—nymphs, satyrs, cupids—are arrayed in curtained alcoves; a fountain squirts weak jets of water at a prodigiously endowed Poseidon ringed by mermaids; Romanesque columns erupt at random spots from the imitation marble floor. In the center of the lobby a board displays lit photographs of the rooms above. There are fantasy rooms made to look like torture dungeons from old B movies, or like science-fiction space capsules; there are rooms devoted to individual Disney characters: the Pooh room; the Minnie room. Other rooms reproduce actual places, from offices to subway cars. To select a room, you push a button below the picture. The picture goes dark. Then an elevator speeds you to your floor, and blinking bulbs in the carpet point you down the hall to a light flashing urgently above your door, as if imploring you to hurry through before you're locked out forever.

(A curious feature of love hotels is that they are completely keyless. Once the door closes, a faint click can be heard: you are now sealed inside. When you want to leave, you insert bills into a machine near the entrance, and the door unlocks. In love hotels, there is no coming and going, no trips down the hall to the ice machine, no visits to your neighbor's room. You are trapped with your partner in your chosen dreamland until you're ready to step outside again; no second thoughts are permitted.)

Airplane lavatories, minotaurs, ergonomic reclining dental chairs, flying elephants: the hotel, you realize, is a world, boxed into faded compartments that smell like cigarette smoke. Wherever you look—in the lobby alcoves, in the patterned wallpaper, in the carved headboards—you will find replicas of

things real and imagined, terrifying and adorable, that belong
to the world outside, but no matter how long you search there
in The Winter Crane Hotel, you won't find a single Winter
Crane.

❀   ❀   ❀

The pretty tour guide leads the seniors deeper into the forest,
her brass buttons winking as she moves in and out of leaf-
shadow. Her pumps are treacherous here on the path, with
its irregular dips and looping tree roots; and they make her
ankles ache besides. She tries not to look like she's walking carefully. Behind her, the seniors march, sure-footed, tireless. She's
grateful for the peace and quiet after all that talking on the bus.
Today's group is, as always, cheerful and gregarious; they treat
her like a granddaughter. On the drive from site to site some of
the women will offer her food from their bento boxes; some of
the men will flirt harmlessly. She likes them, likes her job, but
the break is welcome. Of course, she can't stay silent forever:
at predesignated points along the trail she's required to stop
and, nearly whispering, as though the Winter Crane might be
waiting around the next bend or behind that mottled clump of
bushes, point out interesting features of the landscape. This has
all been precisely timed and scripted. The tour service knows,
after all, that to lead people on a hike through the woods
without any real hope of ever sighting their quarry, they will be
disappointed; so it's made into a nature trek, offering its own
value. The bird is not forgotten, though: here and there the tour
guide recites parts of the myth, as when they finish crossing a
footbridge above a river famous locally for trout fishing, a spot
perhaps not unlike the one where the River God in the tale

rose up angrily and transformed the Queen of the Moon into a crane. She finds herself getting animated as she recounts the story, maybe even a little carried away; and, looking from face to face, she can see that they're enjoying hearing the familiar tale again too. Then they're off again, down the path. Sometimes the seniors tend to linger, enchanted suddenly like children by the most ordinary thing: a spider suspended between bamboo trunks; a glittering shelf of sunlit rock; a butterfly the crisp color of a fall leaf. She keeps them moving, though. They're on a tight schedule: after the crane hike it's a two-hour drive to Ryuganji, where the dragon painted across the curved ceiling is said to move—a rippling of red scales, a subtle undulation—if viewed with believing eyes while lying supine, head pointing south, on the temple's stone floor.

Diorama: Retirement Party,

White Plains, 1997

"All these strangers in my house," Karmala said, stopping in the doorway. "It's like that weird dream feeling, where everything's— Wait. I do know some people."

Or she thought she did. She thought she spotted, among the guests, faces from her childhood, almost unrecognizable now: a cabal that had conspired to wither and bulge and gray together, disguising themselves with age.

"All right. Here we go."

She pulled Lucas through the living room.

"Remember, don't say anything about my job. To anyone. Just, I work in an office. That's all you know."

"Why would anyone ask about your job?"

"These people have known me since I was little. They'll ask. And they'll be good at it. They know how to solicit data from informants."

"I don't think anybody cares what you do for a living. Except maybe your parents. Which you should tell them. It's nothing to be ashamed of. Or I mean it is but."

"Shut up. And I'm serious: be on your guard." She leaned into the kitchen. "There's my mother."

"I'm going to find a drink somewhere," Lucas said. "I need a prop in my hand so I look like I belong here."

Her mother was injecting pink paste into an olive.

"Hi, Mom."

"Oh! Look who's here. How are you, sweetie?"

"Shouldn't I be asking you that?"

"Yes, well, I asked you first."

"I'm not the one who just got out of the hospital."

"Why won't you answer the question? Is something wrong?"

"I'm just saying I think we should be talking about you. The one who's recovering. It's normal to ask, Mom."

"Okay: you've asked. Now answer my question. How are *you*? Is there something I should know about?" She set the olive aside, started on another.

"You win. I'm fine. Absolutely fine."

"See? That's all I wanted to know. Come here."

She let herself be hugged, remembering her mother frail under hospital sheets to reignite empathy.

"Where's Dad?"

"You'd have to go look. He could be anywhere. Hiding, probably."

"Lucas is here," she said.

"Where? I don't see him here. He's not going to say 'hello'?"

"He's hiding too. He's afraid of you."

"Afraid of an old woman. Tell him to be polite and get in here. He's a guest in our home."

"You're not old."

"I'm not young. My husband is retiring. That makes me old by default. Go get Lucas. Tell him I don't bite. And tell him I just got out of the hospital. Then he'll have to come."

"He knows," she said over her shoulder.

Head bowed, drink in hand, Lucas was huddled with a middle-aged history professor whose name Karmala couldn't remember. His hair had fallen from behind his ear, curtaining his face, but from the woman's touched, consoling look Karmala already knew the expression there: brooding, dark-eyed, theatrically intense, as he complained about Hollywood—a former film student, he'd recently decided, on principle, never to make a film—or about the loss of genuine feeling in modern society. Or possibly about Karmala herself.

"Hi," she said to the history professor. "Sorry." She led Lucas away by his sleeve.

Long and waifish and depleted by myriad sorrows, Lucas was the type that some women—although not Karmala—found irresistible. She'd liked him for something else, something she hadn't been able to put her finger on. She'd recently decided that there'd never been anything to put her finger on in the first place. She'd fooled herself again. The problem with Lucas was that he valued his own suffering so highly, yet he had no sensitivity to the suffering of others.

"My mother said go talk to her."

"Your mother scares me."

"You say that and then you spend an hour telling her your tales of woe." She let go of his sleeve at the kitchen doorway.

"Tales of woe."

"As in 'woe is me.'"

"I know what 'woe' means."

She pushed him into the kitchen and went looking for her father.

No matter what Lucas claimed, she was ninety-nine percent sure he wouldn't actually harm himself once she left him. He treasured his imagined pain too much to spoil everything by making it real. He'd be slouching in someone else's arms inside a week.

She thought she spotted her father going down the hall, but was snatched aside before she could reach him. A silver-haired woman in a kaftan held her at arm's length with both hands and looked her over. She said Karmala wouldn't remember her, but she'd changed her diapers when she was a baby. To help her poor mother. Always so smart for her age. Colicky. Would not stop crying. Drove her mother nearly insane. But smart. And here she was, all grown up. What was she doing now?

"I work in an office," Karmala said.

By the time she got to the hallway her father—if it had been her father—was gone.

She got a drink, pink and carbonated in a plastic cup. Pink liquid, pink paste in olives: since when had her mother become pink-fixated? Was it pre- or post-hospital?

She was stopped by more people she didn't recognize but who seemed to recognize her. She was told how big she'd gotten, as if she were still growing. She looked like her mother, she was told. She looked like her father. She looked like both of them. Nobody said that she looked like neither of them. Or that she looked like herself.

Where were those stuffed olives anyway? There were trays with plastic cups all over the place, but she couldn't find her mother's hors d'oeuvres anywhere.

"Don't look but do you see that guy?" Lucas had come up beside her.

She looked. Liver-spotted skull, red suspenders. He didn't seem like a professor. He seemed like he had wandered in by mistake.

"Who is he?"

"Well now that you've given me away. He's been telling me war stories. I'm not kidding. I asked him how he knew your dad and he said they were army buddies or something. Except he got captured and your dad didn't. Said he never talked about it and then spent ten minutes talking about it. He wouldn't stop. I mean it was interesting, though. Screenwriting material, if I was still doing that. You could build a whole movie around this guy's experience. Better than *The Deer Hunter* because it's true. It just . . . It kept making me feel like he was trying to tell me something. Like the only way to understand life is to get captured and eat dandelions every day."

"I doubt if that was the worst part."

"No, the worst part was that some of his Jap guards were nice guys. Actually nice to him. That, apparently, was the worst part. He can't forgive them for that. Japs. His words, not mine. Imagine air quotes." He told her to imagine them because he refused to actually curl his fingers into quotation marks. He thought they were too literal and therefore devoid of irony.

"Maybe it's good for you to hear about other people's misery. Real misery, not the pretend kind."

"Nice. Thanks." He tapped her cup with his in a toast and stalked off.

Her father had one story about the war in the Pacific: he'd parachuted into Borneo, hoping to contact the tribe there, already, at eighteen, a budding anthropologist, craving fieldwork without knowing yet what fieldwork was. Below him a village. Abandoned, as it turned out. Tools left behind in the dirt. A museum diorama, minus the people. It was the biggest disappointment of his life. That was his story. He never talked about if he'd killed, or whom he'd killed, or how many he'd killed.

Karmala noticed for the first time a wheelchair, half-hidden behind the legs of guests.

"Charlotte." She went over and squatted beside her.

"I've been watching you flit around," said Charlotte. "With my one eye." She had a bandage taped over the other.

"I like it. Very swashbuckling."

"I'm a cyclops here in the corner. Scaring everyone away. See how they all avoid me."

"I hate to tell you this, but they avoided you before the bandage. Your reputation intimidates people."

"It never intimidated you."

"Well, I'm not *people*." She grasped Charlotte's hand.

"My darling." Her one eye was wet but old people's eyes were often wet—*rheumy* was the word—and her expression, anyway, was unsentimental.

"You never call me Karmala. I just realized that."

"It's a lovely name. But I don't think I ever forgave your father for not naming you after me. It was the least he could have done."

"I always pictured you as a spider when I was a kid. Kind of creepy. Because of *Charlotte's Web*. Even though Charlotte—the character Charlotte—was nice."

Her rheumy eye was surveying the room. "Your father doesn't look happy."

Karmala turned, saw her father surrounded by grinning people holding plastic cups.

"Does he ever?"

"Worse than usual, I mean. I think you'd better go rescue him, my darling."

She started across the room. Her father looked the way he always looked around people: skittish, tentative, faintly alarmed. The only time he didn't look this way was with immediate family. Or students. She'd seen him lecture once and had felt first surprised and then furious to see him so amiable and openhearted with a roomful of people she didn't know.

"Well," he'd said after class, when she asked him about it, "I put on my teacher face, and, I don't know, by some inverse Stanislavskian miracle, I actually feel, for the time being at least, like I love them and want nothing more than to teach them. To be there with them."

And this face now, she'd thought: have you put on your father face?

He was making his escape from the grinning cup holders. She followed him into his study.

"Dad."

"You made it."

"Me and Lucas. Sorry. I sort of had to bring him." Her parents thought Lucas was hopeless and liked him anyway. They found his endless self-glamorizing travails sad and funny. His suffering was his charm, and he knew it.

"I'm sure that's not true, but don't apologize."

She closed the study door.

"A retirement present." She took out the bag of mushrooms and handed it to him. "Since I can't afford to buy you a ticket to the Place Beyond Culture. Wherever that is."

It had been her father's cruel joke: "Once you're old enough to leave home, I'm gone. Some lost culture. Or better yet someplace where there's no culture at all."

The first time she heard this, back in grade school, she'd felt a sudden dread, even though she knew he was just teasing.

"You're not going anywhere," she'd said, affecting a tone

of weary knowledge. "You guys are staying right here. In this house. Definitely."

"Well, don't worry. *I'm* not going anywhere," her mother had said with a laugh. And she'd felt a second surge of apprehension at the thought that her parents could joke so easily about splitting up.

He held the bag up to the light. "Don't tell your mother."

"She's going to know. She always knows when you're high."

"I mean don't tell your mother it's from you."

"How is she anyway? She wouldn't answer me when I asked."

"She's as well as can be expected." He had opened the bag and was inspecting a mushroom.

"What does that even mean?"

"It means she's fine. More or less. She's recovering. She gets tired easily. And irritable. Very irritable."

"Don't eat all of them. I was told one is more than enough."

"No, no. This is for social purposes. Or I should say communal purposes."

Months before, he'd asked her if she could find him magic mushrooms. "It's no longer the sort of thing you can ask your students to share with you," he'd said. "That sort of thing is frowned on now."

He set the bag on his desk. "I need something to put these in." He circled the room, past the familiar eyeless stare of his hanging masks, lifting things from the clutter and putting them down. "A bowl. Wooden, preferably. But your mother might be in the kitchen."

"What were you doing in here anyway? This is your retirement party. Shouldn't you be out there celebrating?"

"Should be, would be, could be. You and Lucas: same as always, I presume?"

"Yeah. That's the whole problem. But stop using me as an alibi. An excuse to hide in here. Get out there. Those people, they're here for you."

"I can't talk to my own daughter?"

"You can talk to me anytime." She opened the door.

"Jesus."

"H. Christ," she finished. His favorite curse. She grabbed him as he started through the door. "And don't go find Stuart or somebody and just hide in a corner."

"Okay, okay. I'm going. Anything to get away from you."

She grabbed him again. "And talk to Charlotte. She's just sitting there by herself."

"She's probably taking mental notes of everything. Research. Can't you go say hello to her?"

"I already did. I complimented her on her pirate patch."

"It's not like you do it once and then you're off the hook. You're never off the hook. You mingle. Talk to people. Talk to them again."

"That's funny coming from you."

"See, you're the same as me. Exactly like me. That's not fatherly pride. It's a criticism. But I don't accept that it's just my influence. I refuse to feel guilty about you being antisocial. I always hid my tendencies. I would speak to people, complete strangers, just so you would see it and learn. When you were little I made you—"

"Dad. I know what you're doing. Go. Go away. Shoo."

She hated hearing him say they were alike. Not only because of the flaws she saw in him. It made her feel *assembled*. As if everything she'd always considered her character, her own unique self, was really just her parents' scribbles across a *tabula rasa*. Or the genuine Karmala, if there was one, buried beneath, unrecoverable . . .

She left the room, thought of the mushrooms on the desk, and closed the door behind her.

When she was growing up, her father would sometimes smoke weed in the house with his students when her mother wasn't around. Once she'd come home from school and nobody was there. She found her father out in the sauna he'd had built in the backyard. He called it his sweat lodge. He and his students were inside. They were talking, but they weren't making any sense.

"It's kind of like truth or dare," her father explained to her. "Except we're daring ourselves."

"To do what?"

"To reveal things about ourselves we didn't know before we said them."

"Doesn't that make it truth or truth?"

"You want to join us?"

"No," she said. "It sounds boring." Even then—at eight or nine or however old she was—the idea of sitting around revealing things about yourself didn't strike her as appealing.

Much later, when she was a college student, she'd reminded her father of that day. "You were all on something, weren't you? I mean not just weed."

"If you and I are remembering the same incident, I'd been teaching my students about the varieties of Native American religious experience and the assistance of psychotropic allies. Allies: what a great Castanedan word. Remember his books? I used to read them to you before bed."

"Yeah. Other kids get fairy tales. I got anthropology."

"Although as it turned out those books were more fairy tale than anthropology. We didn't know that then, of course. But the point is . . . What was the point? Ah: peyote buttons.

Nobody had any. But one of my students provided the means for us to conduct our own informal pharmacological fieldwork. LSD if I'm not mistaken."

"I thought you guys were crazy."

"I remember having some kind of peak experience. The sort of genuine sweat-lodge-mystical-journey kind of thing you hope for. I remember having it. I just can't remember what I learned. Either that or I imagined it all. That's the problem: all the things you learn along the way, the supposed insights—they're only good for the moment you're having them. You can't save them up and use them later. You look in the bag you've been carrying around your whole life and it's empty."

"Wow," she'd said. "That's reassuring, Dad."

She drifted through the living room. Into the dining room.

"Karmala. My God. Come here, you."

She let herself be hugged. "I see you were talking to Charlotte," she said.

"We must pay homage. On bended knee."

"What does she think about the tattoos anyway?" Stuart had a Morse code of dots and dashes across his face, part of an initiation ceremony when he was a young ethnologist doing fieldwork with some long-lost tribe or other. The only thing left of them, as far as Karmala knew, was in Stuart's writings and on his face. "Does she approve?"

"I've never asked but no would be my guess. Not a prudish grandmother kind of thing, probably. I just don't think she ever approved of my going native, as she saw it."

"Must be nice about the tattoos though, these days. You don't stand out anymore."

He made a mournful face, dots and dashes shifting. When she was little he'd done it deliberately for her, tricks to ripple the patterns. "You'd think so. But, well, first of all, I liked standing out, truth be told. And maybe I still do stand out, but for the wrong reasons. People think I'm some bizarre old fogey trying desperately to keep up. I might as well have a Mohawk and a safety pin in my nose, or, I don't know, whatever it is now. Flannel shirt and ponytail."

"That *would* be desperate. That was like five years ago, but yeah. Anyway, *I* always liked your tattoos."

"Thank you. By the twenty-first century everyone will have one, and then where I will be? For your generation, they've become an initiation ceremony into what exactly? Enlighten me. Not adulthood, surely. You have other rituals for that."

"You're asking the wrong person. I don't have one."

"Yet." He started away, a meandering shuffle, drink in hand. Turned. "It will be legally mandated, mark my words."

"Resist!" She raised a fist in the air.

"Ah, Karmala: ever the contrarian."

She found another drink. You mingle. Talk to people. Talk again. She tried. She felt like she was impersonating herself. If she were working, she could do it easily. She would be incognito as Karmala, or as the Karmala they all expected her to be. She worked for a consulting firm that provided demographic microcultural analysis for corporations. Basically, she did undercover anthropological fieldwork and reported her findings to companies so they could do a better job selling people things. She never knew what happened to these reports but liked to imagine them safeguarded somewhere, conserved for the future in impenetrable corporate hard drives. She'd infiltrated reading circles, support groups, a cosplay convention for obscure retro anime characters—fanged, emerald-haired, she'd been Wairudo Furawa, interdimensional warrior princess—

and, most recently, a meeting of Neo-Luddites convinced the information superhighway would bring about a nightmarish Orwellian future ending in civilization's demise. (It was one of the Neo-Luddites—this was the nickname she and her coworkers used at the office; the Neo-Luddites didn't actually call themselves that—who had sold her the mushrooms.) The hardest part of her job was not pretending to be someone else. That was the part she liked. The hardest part was the preparatory research. You didn't just walk into a closed microculture and wing it. She'd given herself away only once, her first time in the field, at a national Pi Beta Phi alumnae gathering. Not because she hadn't sufficiently prepped, but because she was too nosy, too overtly curious with her informants.

She wasn't sure if she was ashamed to tell her parents because of the whole anthropological-methods-for-evil-corporate-ends part, or because, career-wise, even after studying theater in college and communication theory in graduate school, she'd ended up following in her father's footsteps in spite of herself . . .

And where did those footsteps lead? To a lifetime spent trying to capture and hold fragile things before they collapsed. She saw in her mind Stuart's loosening net of dots and dashes, its code dimming across his features into indecipherability.

What she really needed, Karmala decided, was a break from this party's gallery of ruined faces. This sad trip down memory lane. She could hide in her room for a while. That was one place that hadn't changed since childhood. Her parents had protected it from ruin or practical utility by keeping it exactly as it had been the day she left home.

She went upstairs. If she did get a tattoo: what symbol to summarize her life? Her personality? Not to mention the question of where. Reveal or conceal or peek-a-boo?

Hushed voices argued on the other side of her bedroom door. She put her ear against it: a man and woman were debating the merits of one of Charlotte's early books. They both hated it, for different reasons. She opened the door, preparing indignation at these trespassers into her private space. They stared from the bed, her father's graduate students most likely, clothes scattered across her Shanna the She-Devil blanket. After the shock left their faces they replaced it with their own look of indignation.

"If you want to criticize Charlotte, why don't you go tell her all about it? I'm sure she'd love to hear your opinions." She closed the door, opened it. "And get off my bed."

She went downstairs.

A man came out of the study with one of her father's masks on.

"Dad. Should I be concerned?"

He said something, muffled by the mask. He took it off.

"Only if you want to be. There's always cause for concern."

"Okay."

"The looming darkness."

"Thanks, Dad."

"Ultimately we choose how to face the terror. Or if we face it."

"Words of wisdom. I shouldn't have given you the mushrooms."

"I haven't even taken any. Well, one. Half of one. No effect. I'm still waiting. I think we all are. There's a communal bowl in the study if you want to partake. What was I talking about?"

"Terror. You can put the mask back on."

"That's the first time you've said that. You were always screaming for me to take it off."

"Because it was terrifying. Since we're talking about terror. Chasing a five-year-old around the house with a mask on."

"It was fun. It was supposed to be fun. Kids love masks. Halloween. Or *Setsubun.* The Japanese father, pursuing his children in a demon mask until they throw beans at him and he's cast out. Then the home is purified."

"You never gave me any beans. Just ran around the house in a mask without any clothes on."

"You're conflating two memories. I prefer to sleep naked. For which I feel no need to apologize. I get up to use the bathroom. Perfectly natural. If we'd all been born somewhere else . . . I had hoped I could save you from cultural brainwashing, but I should have known better. Don't tell Charlotte I called it brainwashing. It goes against everything she taught me. Where is she anyway? I don't see her in her corner."

"Maybe she found the mushrooms."

Over on the couch, Lucas was with the POW again. Listening, puffy-eyed, as the old man talked. Not just puffy-eyed; Lucas was crying, she realized. Crying. For all his moping, she'd never seen him cry before. She felt outraged, as if at a betrayal . . .

Her father was gone.

She wandered from room to room. She had the feeling that she was looking for something important, but couldn't remember what it was. She stopped, leaned against a wall.

What right did Lucas have, crying like that? Showing a face like that?

She drank from her cup. She wondered what the POW was saying to Lucas. It occurred to her that she'd never really asked her father questions about his life. He'd told her what he wanted to. And until now that had been enough . . . Stuart, her father, the prisoner of war: in twenty years that generation would be gone. A vanishing breed . . . Gone: she was seized by a panic to act. To save her father from extinction. Why hadn't she tried harder to find out more about him? Still, it wasn't too late. She could conduct an interview, her father as her informant. Create an oral history of his hidden life, carried out clinically, like the reports she prepared at work. Everything important preserved there. But she already knew she wouldn't do it. She would end up getting distracted by something. She would forget.

She looked around, trying again to spot the transformed faces of people she'd known once, but didn't recognize anyone now. A vanishing breed. She saw her father vanishing into the Place Beyond Culture, which she pictured as vaguely heavenly, soft-sided and featureless like a vast padded room. Although maybe she was picturing that Catholic place: Purgatory. Or was it Limbo? Because what features could there be, after all, in a Place Beyond Culture?

But if she was going to worry about one of her parents vanishing into Limbo, shouldn't she be worried about her mother? And thinking this, she did worry, again, a feeling that always felt more like guilt. Guilt for insufficient worrying . . .

Her mother's hors d'oeuvres. That was what she'd been looking for. She went hunting. She was determined to find them. On an end table, she finally located a tray full of the stuffed olives. She picked it up, carrying it with her, plopping one olive in her mouth at a time as she walked. She really had no idea what the pink paste was. All these people . . . She walked and plopped, two at a time, three, filling her mouth. All these people here to honor her father.

She set the empty tray on a chair. She was ready to go, once she found Lucas, missing from the couch now, along with the prisoner of war. She had done her duty by this point. Stayed long enough. She would tell her parents she had work to do over the weekend and needed to head back to the city. Which was true: she had research for her next undercover assignment. Plus she didn't want to stay too long, or the acquaintances and strangers would all leave and only her parents and their close friends would be left. It could all get awkward. And then her parents would insist she and Lucas stay overnight. She thought of the Charlotte-debating grad students fucking on her Shanna the She-Devil blanket. So there was that too. All good reasons to go.

Her mother was in a dining room chair, watching the guests. "Have you seen Dad?" Karmala asked, trying to decide if her mother looked more tired than usual.

"I haven't seen him, or anyone else I know. Everyone's gone missing. Who are these people in my house?"

"Can you say goodbye for me? And congratulations and everything. We've got to go."

"You can say it yourself. You know how he'd feel if you just left without a proper goodbye. He's here somewhere."

Except he wasn't. She went upstairs, past people sitting or standing on the steps. Downstairs, into the study. He wasn't there. Neither were his mushrooms.

She realized where he was. She went through the house. Strangers everywhere. On her patio too, cigarette ends wavering like fireflies, voices confidential. She walked past them, out onto the lawn. The grass was blue under the starlight. The sweat lodge a dense black oblong. She opened the door.

There they were, the whole Vanishing Breed. None of them had any clothes on. Just her father's masks. She was thankful for the steam.

"Karmala. Finally. Close the door and grab a mask. It'll do you good. The bowl is over there on the bench."

She couldn't tell where the voice was coming from. The mask her father had been wearing was there, but it was atop the body of a flabby woman now. Steam drifted, hiding and revealing faces. She remembered them all from childhood: the curly-mustached green face with the earrings and the dot between the eyebrows; the slit-eyed face circled in fur; the long face from her nightmares with the striped cheeks and the O for a mouth; the straw-haired Protector . . . She recognized all of the faces, but had no idea which one belonged to her father.

Ichiban

Daiji was a college student when he first began to receive specific and more or less reliable information about the night world. On Monday mornings his classmates would recount for him their weekend exploits in Tokyo's neon labyrinth: he heard about soaplands, where you were bathed in bubbly mountains of suds, then treated to sex right there on the slippery mat; and image clubs, where your chosen partner came to you as a stewardess, or as a nurse, or as a bride, or in any other costume you could imagine. And he heard about hostess clubs, where women as beautiful as TV actresses drank with you at your own private table. He heard about all these places, his friends educating him with a smirking, embarrassed bravado he secretly despised. But Daiji couldn't afford to experience the night world firsthand. That, at least, was what he would tell his classmates when they invited him along on one of their drunken adventures.

After college he was too busy with work to let himself think about the pleasures available to him now that he had a good salary. He didn't want to be distracted. Then also there was the habit of self-denial he had learned in all the years he had spent studying for high school and college entrance exams. He had taught himself that rewards were things to be postponed. (Once

117

he got as far as the mirrored door of "The Shining Empire," but then, confronted by his own earnestly frowning reflection, spun around and hurried away.)

It wasn't until after he was married that Daiji started to explore Tokyo's night world for himself. He would patiently set aside money from the small allowance given to him by his wife, practicing every possible austerity, exercising nearly ascetic restraint, to create another, even smaller allowance, with which he awarded himself a clandestine monthly visit to a pleasure palace. What he discovered was this: he didn't like sex clubs. They made him feel exposed and ugly. Taking off his clothes in front of the girl was bad enough; but some insisted on helping him, smilingly unbuttoning his dress shirt (the last button was the worst), to reveal a quivering expanse of flab, like some awful present that should never have been opened. They might not have cared—anyway if they did they were always tactful enough not to show it—but *he* cared. Also, something about sex with a stranger felt wrong. Maybe it was because there was no flirtation, no pretense of romantic interest. Anyway he left these places feeling worse than when he had entered.

He found, to his surprise, that he preferred the hostess clubs, although there was no sex on offer at all. Instead, a seemingly endless parade of women joined him, one at a time, in a secluded booth. They knew how to talk to him. If he disparaged himself because of his weight or appearance, he was told that a heavy build and "frank" features were "signs of a *real* man"; and the hostess would go on to make fun of the angular, effeminate pretty boys so common in Japan today, the kind who spent their free time at the tanning salon or in front of the mirror plucking eyebrows. If, when asked his age, he sheepishly replied that he was thirty-five ("Basically over the hill, right?"), his partner would tell him she preferred older men: they were more mature and experienced. He knew, of course, that they were flattering him, and he soon realized that the women had all been taught the same soothing repertoire. It didn't matter. Every time Daiji went to one of these clubs a stylized and abbreviated courtship was enacted. But, unlike a real courtship, it was rendered stress-free—by the professional skills of the women, and by the knowledge that they were, after all, only pretending.

If there was one thing that bothered him, it was the anxious wait at the table before the hostess arrived. He sat there, inert, helpless. The club's invisible manager—like some fickle god who spoke only through his emissaries, the waiters—sent you a partner, and there was never any way to predict what sort of woman he would elect to confer upon you. For another five thousand yen you could, it was true, request the partner of your choice; but Daiji was on a strict budget, and he had never found anyone he liked so much that he was willing to exceed his allowance just to have her sit beside him again.

When, one night, he did finally make a request, it was for a woman he had never even met.

He was being shown to his seat when she swept past, a graceful figure in a silk cocktail dress. He caught only a glimpse: black hair, a pale throat, a face in profile. But it was enough. He thought: I hope someone like *that* comes to my table. Send me a good one tonight. And at first, when a hostess approached— his eyes registering a cascade of bronze curls and a skirt slit practically to the waist—he believed the manager had in fact favored him this evening. But then she sat down beside him, coming within the effective range of his vision, and he saw a plain face, coated with a layer of makeup which didn't quite hide the furious red pimple on her chin . . .

The girl wouldn't stop talking. She was a cheerfully self-absorbed monologuist, jabbering on obliviously in some rustic dialect she made no effort to correct.

"How about you?" she asked.

"What?" When he had stopped listening, about five minutes before, she had been fondly complaining about her hometown.

"Do you live in Tokyo?"

"No, in Saitama. I commute."

"Me too!" she shrieked, grabbing his arm. "I commute too! It's terrible, isn't it?" She beamed at him with grateful fellow feeling, as if she had at long last found the one other person capable of understanding the trials of commuting to Tokyo every day.

He thought of the money he was wasting, and of the month-long wait before he would be able to come here again. When were they going to bring him someone new? He looked around the room, trying to make out the other prospects. Without his glasses, though, their faces were smudged featureless ovals. He always kept his glasses in his briefcase when he was at one of these clubs. They destroyed the fun-loving, carefree image he wanted to project.

"Who is that over there?"

"Hmm? Which one?"

"Second from the right. In the purple dress."

The figure was hazy, but he thought it might be the woman he had glimpsed earlier.

"Purple dress? *Oh.* With her hair up? That's Reina. Our Number One."

Number One. He refused to feel awe at the words. Tokyo's most popular hostesses enjoyed a special status. If TV dramas were to be believed, they led glamorous lives, vacationing on yachts and island resorts and sometimes bringing in more, between their salary and the gifts they received, than their wealthiest customers. Not that he bought into all that non-sense. In the end, they were just girls, after all, fundamentally no different than the one beside him right now.

"Is she your type?" the girl teased, giggling to show him she felt no jealousy or rivalry.

"I don't know. I mean, I can't really see from over here. I passed her when I came in and she looked . . . What's she like?"

"Reina? She's . . . very pretty. Do you want to invite her over?"

Invite her over? "No! Well. If— Would I be able to spend much time with her? Or would she be so busy . . . ?"

"Well, she might have to come and go, you know, if other customers request her. But tonight's pretty quiet, so prob-ably . . ."

And then, without really being sure what he was doing, he had gotten another five thousand yen tacked onto his bill for the privilege of having the club's Number One sit next to him.

"It's very brave," the girl said after she put in his request with one of the waiters.

"What is?"

"Calling her over without ever having talked to her."

"By 'brave' you mean 'strange'?"

"No." She patted his hand reassuringly. "It's not strange. Just a little unusual. Because, you know, most men only request girls they've talked to before. That way they're sure they'll get along."

"I hope I haven't made a mistake . . ."

"Are you nervous?" She giggled again.

"A little, maybe . . ."

"But it's exciting, isn't it?"

And then a waiter came and called her away, and a moment later the club's Number One stood over him.

"May I?" She gestured to the space beside him.

"Oh. Yes. Please."

She sat down. From her purse she produced a card case. From the case she produced a business card. She presented it to him with both hands, bowing. "My name is Reina Aihara. It's a pleasure to meet you."

As he accepted the card and stuck it in his breast pocket he looked her over.

Certainly she was pretty. She had sharp features set precisely in a pale round face. And there was what he had noticed when she passed him earlier: a slender, long-necked elegance, accentuated by the way her black hair was swept up into a perfect bun shaped like a seashell. Also, she had lovely, apparently poreless skin; if she wore makeup it was applied so subtly he couldn't see it. Still, he felt faintly disappointed. For example, take that perfect skin. In a world where the women hid themselves behind a camouflage of dye jobs and hair extensions, color contacts and false eyelashes (not to mention the multihued splotches painted across their faces), her willingness to lay herself bare could be seen as courageous, but it could also imply an arrogant indifference to presentation. She might not *need* to wear makeup, but shouldn't she put it on anyway, as a sign of respect to the customer? Then there was her smile. It happened on only one side of her face. The effect was so extreme that at first he suspected partial paralysis: one corner of her mouth rose up cooperatively enough; the other seemed to strain a little, but stayed right where it was.

She asked the typical questions about his life. Was he married? Yes. Did he have any children? No: not yet. What kind of work did he do? He worked in the dividend reinvestment department of a bank. She nodded with equal emphasis to every reply. He found himself mentioning, as if in passing, that he was a Tokyo University graduate. She made appropriate little awed sounds, and told him he must be very bright; but she didn't *look* awed, and she didn't treat him differently, the way people usually did . . . He even pulled back his sleeve, ostensibly to check the time, displaying the silver Rolex his parents had given him as a college graduation present. But she only said:

"Do you have to go now? Should I call for the check?"

Her cool formality started to bother him. The more he drank, the more it bothered him. He switched to plain Japanese, hoping it would encourage her to follow suit. She kept right on using honorific language, her words, like her manner, dignified and aloof. He sounded like a brute by comparison. But it was too late to go back to formal Japanese now. He soldiered on. He was drinking too much, he knew; he would be drunk soon. If he wasn't already. It was all making him nervous, which made him drink more. And she kept obligingly refilling his glass from the decanter on the table.

And another thing: she didn't touch his knee or his hand or his arm when she talked. She wasn't flirting with him at all! How could this be the Number One?

Or maybe it was him. Maybe she just didn't like him.

This thought had a temporarily sobering effect. His scalp went cold and seemed to shrink around his skull. Still, he was paying, wasn't he? He was the customer here. There was no need to fawn all over her.

The man at the next table was giving his hostess a neck massage; her ecstatic moans suggested he was an expert masseur.

At another table a guy was clasping the wrist of his partner and playing some sort of game with her fingers while she laughed hysterically. All around him, it seemed, paired figures nestled closer, inclining heads, merging fuzzily as they murmured to each other in the secretive voices lovers use.

"So," he heard himself blurt, cutting her off in mid-sentence, "tell me: do you have a boyfriend or what?"

"No." She dabbed daintily with her handkerchief at the condensation on his glass. "Not anymore."

He instantly regretted the question. He must really be drunk, to ask something like that. What an idiot he was. Reverting to formal Japanese, he said: "I'm terribly sorry. I shouldn't have asked that. It was—please forgive me."

"No, it's all right."

"I'm sorry, it's just, well, you're very pretty and it seems odd, no, not odd, but surprising that you—"

"Really, it's all right." She paused. "We broke up last year. He couldn't stand not being able to see me more. With this kind of work, it's hard to have a relationship. And for me, now, my job comes first. I'm trying to save money, so I'm putting all my energy into it."

"I respect that. I think that's wonderful."

He was about to ask her what she was saving for, but the waiter had come. He knelt and held out the leather folder containing the check. Daiji's time was up.

In the past, after he paid, the girl beside him would always ask for his cell phone number and email address. But now the Number One was escorting him to the door, and she still hadn't said a word. He couldn't wait any longer.

"Do you think we could exchange contact information?" he asked.

❀   ❀   ❀

The lights were all off in his apartment. He closed the door quietly, in case his wife had gone to bed. Then he slipped out of his shoes, and moved tentatively forward in the darkness.

A silvery light pulsed in the living room. His wife was sitting on the floor in her enormous pajamas. Hunched there in the dark before the TV screen, she looked to him for an instant like some nocturnal animal gazing up at the light of the moon.

"I'm home," he said.

A sharp hand shot out of her sleeve and silenced him with a wave. On the TV a woman was giving a tearful account of some domestic nightmare or other. To conceal her identity, her face had been blurred and her voice electronically altered to sound like Minnie Mouse.

He stood there awkwardly, briefcase in hand, waiting for the commercial. They had been married for more than three years now, but she was still able to make him feel like an unwelcome visitor in his own home.

Courtship and marriage had not come easily to him. It had all been an ordeal that he had miraculously survived. After college, he had thought he might meet someone in his office. He was, after all, the assistant to the submanager, and well known to everyone as "that guy from Tokyo University." But the women he worked with showed no interest in him. He watched them pair off with men in the office who had lower salaries and mediocre educational backgrounds. At twenty-seven he started to attend special parties organized for Tokyo University graduates and the women hoping to marry them. These were always ritzy affairs held in the banquet halls of the best hotels. The graduates mingled with stewardesses, models, and executive secretaries. Daiji marveled at the screening that must have been necessary to get only the best-educated and most beautiful prospective wives. But while his fellow graduates swooped down on their prey, bragging about jobs and cars and vacations abroad until the moment when, with a triumphant flourish, they could flip open their cell phones and deftly enter the women's contact information, Daiji stood alone at a table munching forlornly on hors d'oeuvres and wondering what he could possibly use as an opening line. He knew he shouldn't have to worry about this: he was a Tokyo University graduate, one of the elite, and these women were here to shop for men just like him. He had nothing to prove. But the end of these events always found him slumping home alone, dreading the inevitable inquiring call from his mother.

Finally, after his thirty-second birthday, his mother made it clear that she and his father didn't intend to wait any longer. A matchmaker was arranged for. She was a friend of his mother, a squat ruddy woman who had known Daiji since he was a boy, although he couldn't recall ever having spoken to her. Now she spread the forms out on the table with ceremonial care, as if laying out tarot cards. Her face, too, had the hokey solemnity of a soothsayer. Each form had a photo pasted into a space in the upper right corner. He scanned the pieces of paper, pretending to scrutinize the educational histories and work backgrounds of his potential future wives, while secretly letting his eyes stray to the little color photos. They were serious-faced women, all of them, staring back at him with the blank, composed look people have when their pictures are taken at the Department of Motor Vehicles. He had expected better candidates. He was a graduate of Japan's number one university, wasn't he? Not that they were ugly, but he couldn't help thinking of the wives of his former classmates (all of whom were married by now); they seemed to be of a different class. Could it have something to do with the gap between high school and college on his curriculum vitae? Daiji had, it was true, failed the National Exam the first time. And as a result, he had spent twelve months in limbo, studying and worrying and waiting until he could try again the following winter. But did that one failure mean he wasn't entitled to the best? The matchmaker wouldn't say this in so many words. But he started to feel in her frustrated insistence that these were perfectly nice girls who would make wonderful wives a hint that he shouldn't be aiming any higher, that his year in limbo effectively barred his entry to a better world. He became convinced that there were higher-class candidates—more beautiful, more sophisticated—that she was keeping from him. Accept reality, she seemed to be saying. Finally he agreed to meet one of the women in the photos . . .

The matchmaker, who had been pushy and maternal throughout the selection process, telling him authoritatively who would be best for him and why, seemed now to have lost her voice. She sat anxiously in her kimono at the end of the table while they all took perfunctory sips of green tea, he and the girl and both of their mothers. He had to admit it: the girl was, as the matchmaker had promised, better than her picture. Not beautiful, but above average, definitely. Her face was pleasant, and she came from a good family, and she was talkative, which annoyed him at first, but certainly made things easier for him on their dates, since he didn't have to endure awkward silences: she would always fill those spaces with some kind of small talk. There was nothing at all wrong with her. On their fifth date, they went to a love hotel—she suggested it matter-of-factly as they drove past the fairy-tale-castle spire of the HappyTime Inn—and she was sweetly understanding when he got overexcited and spurted all over her thigh before anything had even really begun. He felt that he loved her then—for accepting him, for not making him feel ridiculous.

His proposal set in motion a complex and mysterious machine, and before he knew it he and his new bride were bowing together in the dark wooden gleam of a shrine, gold panels dancing around them, while the priest, a young man with the face of a predatory bird, intoned blessings in a whining voice and shook zigzags of the purest white paper over their heads.

"Dinner's in the fridge," his wife said when the commercial finally came. "You can heat it in the microwave."

He went into the kitchen, opened the refrigerator, and then realized he was still holding his briefcase. He set it down and gazed into the cheerily lit box at bowls shrouded in translucent plastic wrap. He wasn't hungry, really; in fact his stomach felt a little upset.

What he really needed was a bath to calm him down. As he undressed and started the bathwater, he remembered the way his mother always had dinner and a hot bath ready for his father when he came home. His mother might not have been the sweetest wife, but she was a dutiful one. No one could take that away from her. Speaking of duties, he hadn't called his parents in over a month. His mother would be feeling neglected. But he could already imagine the first words out of her mouth (after scolding him for not calling more). They were the same words she said every time he called: "Is she pregnant yet?" Producing a child: the next test for him to pass. There was no way to tell his mother that his present relationship with her daughter-in-law made it physically impossible to give her the grandchild she kept demanding.

When he thought of his mother he often felt annoyance. Annoyance, and an obscure guilt. But now another feeling came over him—or maybe it had been there all along and he was just now noticing it—and it was so unfamiliar that at first he didn't recognize the feeling for what it was.

He sat on the tub's edge listening to the roar of the water and gazing at his soft white legs splayed on the tile. It had never occurred to him that he was unhappy. If someone had asked him if he was satisfied with his life he would have said, "Sure, I'm as happy as anyone, I guess." He never would have thought he had anything to be especially unhappy about. But now it seemed to him that the things that filled his life fell short.

The tub was nearly overflowing. He turned off the faucet. Gingerly he dipped a foot into the steaming water (he had made it almost too hot), then stepped inside, one leg after the other, bracing himself against the rim of the tub and cautioning himself that he was still a little drunk. Cupping his hands over his crotch, he slowly lowered himself to a squat.

He had hoped for more when he was young. Everyone did. There was nothing special in that. But not everyone graduated at the top of his high school class. Not everyone got into the nation's best university. Hadn't he earned the right to hope for more?

The fact was, he had settled for second-best. In his job, certainly: it was the kind of work his mother had called "dependable." And his marriage? His marriage was like his job: it had seemed challenging and hopeful in the beginning, but had turned out to be neither; instead, it was a routine that maintained itself as long as he put in the effort of showing up every day.

He had settled for second-best in his life.

But should he be blaming himself? Hadn't he been led to

believe that, with hard work and a good education, something more would be waiting for him? He scooped up a handful of water and splashed it over his clenched face. How could he blame himself when he had done everything he was supposed to do?

By the time he climbed out of the tub he wasn't sad anymore. Instead, he felt . . . outraged. As if he had been wronged. As if he were the victim of a broken promise.

This feeling remained as he dried himself off and walked through the dark apartment. The television was off. His wife had gone to bed without saying good night. In the bedroom he heard her snoring wheezily from under a mound of covers. He crawled in beside her, making the bed rock more than was necessary and rustling the sheets. But she slept on, snored on.

For a long time he lay on his back, unable to shake the sense that a promise had been broken. He felt almost sick. The main thing was to keep everything from moving. He lay very still. His mind, too, needed to be stilled. But the thought was there. A promise had been broken. The words seemed to turn and turn above him like the chirping birds that crown the injured heads of characters in children's cartoons. They circled dizzyingly, accompanied by the music of his wife's snoring.

❄   ❄   ❄

Daiji stared at his phone's empty square, his thumb poised above the keypad. Occasionally the thumb twitched nervously, but otherwise it didn't move. He had started and erased two text messages. Now he couldn't decide what to write. He couldn't decide whether he should be writing anything at all.

When he checked his mail the morning after going to the

club, he had expected a message from the Number One. In the past, when he gave a hostess his email address, she could always be counted on to compose for him a cute little text message right after she finished her shift, thanking him in a cryptic baby talk interspersed with the hearts and stars and smiley faces teenage girls put in as if in some new system of punctuation. But this time there was nothing. He waited another day. Nothing. He told himself he would wait one more day and then forget about her. She had said she would contact him; he may have been drunk, but he remembered that clearly. Still, she *was* Number One. Maybe she expected the customer to do the contacting. Maybe it was a kind of test. If so, what arrogance! What made her so different from the other women? The answer was simple: she was the most popular one in the club. If she had come to expect special treatment, there was nothing he could do about that. He either accommodated her, or . . . And if she *was* waiting for a message, he should send it soon. He had let three days slip by already. She might think he was rude. Or uninterested.

He went into the office bathroom and locked himself in a stall. *Hello Reina.* All right: but what next? It was best to keep it simple: just thank her for the other evening. He keyed in and immediately erased this message. The point was this: *he* was the customer. Shouldn't she be thanking him? In his second message he asked her how she was; he said he was worried, since he hadn't heard . . . No. It sounded angry and desperate.

His thumb twitched. He stared at the display.

He had been in here on the stool for too long; people would start to wonder what had happened to him. All right. His thumb came down onto the pad decisively. *Hello Reina. Sorry to be so late in writing to you. Thank you for the other night. I had a wonderful time. I hope I can see you again.* And without giving himself a chance to change his mind, he selected SEND.

Two days later she sent him a brief and very polite message thanking him for his email and for visiting the club. He read it five times, then sent a reply, thanking her for thanking him for his email, and asking if he might have the honor of inviting her to his table again the next time he visited the club. This time she answered almost immediately, telling him *she* was the one who would be honored. And then, attached to the end of the message, came the inconsequential personal comment that passed through him like a tremor, leaving everything in its wake gaping and shattered: *I'm so tired . . . After I finish this message I'm going to take a nice long bath.*

He started to check for messages five or six times a day. Although everyone in the office sent and checked mail during work hours, he found himself hiding his cell phone under the desk like a schoolboy using it to cheat on an exam . . . When, in one message, she warned him to take care because a typhoon was coming, he was touched at her concern, although he knew perfectly well that what she had written was nothing more than a formulaic expression. And when, in another message, she mentioned attending a friend's wedding, and wondered whether she would ever get married herself, he felt his chest constrict with a horrible mixture of desire and regret.

❁   ❁   ❁

At the door he requested Reina. The doorman bowed and ushered him inside.

The place was busier than it had been the time before, and almost half of his one-hour set passed before the Number One was able to come to his table. Daiji kept squinting, craning his neck, trying to distinguish her blurry shape from all of the others. After an initial attempt at conversation, the girl beside him had given up and, stiffening, primly withdrawn the knee that had been touching his. She gazed silently into her lap, where she clutched a damp flowered handkerchief. Every thirty seconds or so, the girl used the handkerchief to wipe away nonexistent condensation from his glass. Finally she was called away and the Number One took her place.

"Thank you so much for asking to see me," she said, bowing.

The first time he met her this cool formality had unnerved him; this time, though, he had the memory of her text messages, and this changed everything: her most banal words seemed now to be perfumed with a secret meaning only he could detect . . .

"I'm glad you remembered me," she said.

"How could I forget?" he said, smiling. The way these words came to his service impressed him (where had they come from?). The result was impressive too: she blushed and shyly averted her eyes.

"Are you surprised to see me?" he said in an intimate tone, leaning toward her. He wasn't nervous at all! For the first time in his life he felt suave and masterful.

"Yes, very! Surprised and happy."

"I brought you something." He opened his briefcase. "It's nothing special; just a little thing, but . . ."

She looked gravely at the package in his hand before accepting it. The look on her face made him feel like a messenger delivering bad news rather than a suitor offering a token of affection.

She slowly unwrapped the package. Then she opened the

box and took out his gift by its loop of chain, her fingers spread starfish-fashion. A gold pendant in the shape of a heart dangled from the chain. She set it gently on her other hand. Embedded in the heart was a diamond. It had seemed larger in the store; now it resembled a stray speck of glitter, something that could be wiped away with a stroke of her thumb. On her face was a look of pity—she might have been looking at a tiny wounded creature that had landed on her palm.

He felt humiliated. The pendant was cheap. He had been assured that it was real gold—14 karat—and that the diamond was real too. But it was a poor man's present, bought on sale at a discount department store. He couldn't afford anything more with his allowance. He had overextended himself as it was.

"Thank you."

She returned it to the box and quietly put the box in her purse.

"I'm sorry, I don't know your taste, so I—"

"It's very nice. Thank you."

"But you don't like it. I can take it back and get something else if you prefer . . ."

"No, it's not that."

"Was I wrong to give you a present?"

"It's just that, well, to be honest, when men give me things, I feel like they're expecting something in return."

". . . Oh! No! No, I'm not expecting anything. I just gave it because I wanted to, because I wanted to express . . . So no, you know, no strings attached."

"Then thank you."

"So, is it all right? For me to have given you that. I know it wasn't anything much. The problem is, I really don't know what would make you happiest. If you would tell me . . ."

She set an extra ice cube in his drink and stirred it meditatively before answering. "The easiest thing," she said, "would be for us to go shopping together. We can have dinner afterward, and then you can come with me to the club. It'll be a shopping date."

"Really? Yes! Yes, definitely."

A date! Then he thought of something.

"Does it bother you that I'm married?"

She seemed surprised by the question.

"Not at all. I prefer married men. It makes everything less complicated."

❀   ❀   ❀

The problem was money. Or, rather, the problem was his wife. Because his wife controlled the money. In the past, to save for his monthly visit to a club, he would, for instance, occasionally go hungry, skipping a meal (or if he absolutely had to eat, sitting at a counter elbow to elbow with college students and manual laborers, contenting himself with a four-hundred-yen bowl of rice topped with fatty gray meat). He had also found he could shave a little off his commuting expenses if he followed a circuitous route to work and back, changing trains four times each way. But this time none of these measures would be sufficient. There was no telling what the Number One might decide to pick out for herself. And he couldn't risk not having enough money to pay for it. He had to be ready. Credit cards were out of the question, since his wife paid all the bills. He knew there was only one answer, although it took him a week to admit it to himself and to begin devising a plan.

He would have to dip into the special savings account. Every month a portion of his salary was automatically deposited into this account, which, over the last three years, had grown nearly large enough for the deposit on a house. They never touched this account, so she wouldn't notice a temporary withdrawal. Later, he would find a way to replace the money.

This account represented a rare point of agreement between Daiji and his wife. They argued about his mother. They argued about children (he wanted them, or at least felt that he was supposed to; she had, as she put it, "done her best" during the first year of their marriage—although increasingly with stoical distaste, as if at an unavoidable household chore—but she didn't get pregnant, and for a long time now had barely touched him, let alone . . .). They had never, though, argued about getting a house. They both wanted to live in a real home, a place with room to spare, instead of the cramped apartment they shared now, and they were both willing to endure frugal, even meager existences to get it.

On Saturday mornings his wife took an English class at the YWCA. This class was the one luxury she allowed herself, fitting as it did into some absurd dream she maintained of an "international lifestyle." As soon as she left he started his search. Three hours later he found the bank passbook and stamp hidden between the pages of the instruction manual for "Belly Zapper," an electric-stimulation exercise belt which his wife had bought for him after seeing it advertised on TV, and which now languished, neglected, in the bedroom closet.

He arranged to meet the Number One in front of a department store near Tokyo Station. It was a popular meeting place for dates, and when he arrived, fifteen minutes early, the sidewalk was crowded with young men and women. They glanced around nonchalantly or consulted their cell phones, pretending that they weren't waiting for someone's arrival. Standing among them he felt old and ridiculous. What was he doing here anyway? He thought of the Number One, and felt an impulse to leave, to turn and run away while he still could. He told himself if she didn't appear in the next sixty seconds he would go home and never contact her again. After a minute passed he decided to grant her sixty more seconds. He found an unobtrusive spot near the wall in the shadow of a pillar. Here he waited for seven minutes before remembering that he was still wearing his glasses. He snatched them from his face and slid them furtively into his briefcase. Instantly the people around him were replaced by poorly painted watercolor figures. He watched them as they came and went in an enigmatic blurred dance.

One of the figures came near. It was the Number One.

"What are you doing?" she asked. "How long have you been standing here?"

"Oh, not long. I just arrived a few minutes ago myself," he lied, not wanting her to feel bad about being late.

"Didn't you see me? I've been waiting right over there for ten minutes."

"Really?"

He started to bow frantically, bobbing up and down as he spoke. "Sorry!"—bob—"I should have"—bob—"looked more"—bob—"carefully—"

"Never mind . . . So. What should we do now?"

Hadn't they already agreed to go shopping today? Hadn't she called it a "shopping date"?

Then he realized that it was, for some reason he didn't yet understand, necessary for him to say it himself.

"Let's go shopping," he said.

"All right. Do you want me to help you pick out something for yourself?"

"No. No, not for me. For you. Let's go find something for you," he said.

There was that asymmetrical smile again.

They went inside.

"I haven't been here in a long time," she said. "Where should we go?"

They approached a directory. He put his finger on the panel. *Designer goods.* "The second floor?"

"All right."

They found an escalator in the cosmetics section. He rode a corrugated step, the Number One beside him. When they reached the second floor, Daiji suddenly remembered going shopping with his wife in a place like this. They had just gotten married. She had been looking for a new handbag, and, feeling generous, he had told her she should get herself whatever she wanted. But after a few minutes she had said all the shops were too expensive. She had found a bag, some cheap thing, on sale somewhere else.

As he walked down the carpeted aisle with the Number One, he pictured the handbag, badly battered and pitifully unfashionable, but still in use. Five years from now—ten!—his wife would still be carrying it around . . .

On either side of him, above his head, foreign words were lettered in brass or engraved in marble. Below the words were window displays exhibiting necklaces, purses, and dresses, each item lit reverently like a sacred relic. The Number One ignored it all, strolling along at an aimless gait, a dreamy expression on her face.

He wanted her to hurry up and decide on a shop. She had to decide now. It was urgent. Because another part of him was rehearsing excuses, constructing lies, anything to get off the hook and away from her.

They stopped. They were standing before a store's arched entrance. He squinted, but could make out only flashes of gold amid the dark gleam of wood.

"Do you want to take a look inside?" he asked after a moment.

"If you like."

But he didn't move. He was held between forces. Then, mercifully, she took his arm in a gentle guiding action. At her touch his heart began its irrevocable fall away from him, like a ripe fruit from its branch. He understood what he was willing to give for her touch. He understood too that she would not satisfy him, and that he would keep giving anyway.

The Number One drifted through the store. Daiji followed. He asked her what she wanted. She told him he had to choose the gift himself. He begged her to pick her own present, sparing him the risk of failure; but she was resolute. She helped him, though: at times her hand would come to rest on a particular plate of glass; at other times she would pause for a beat in front of a display before moving on. She was teaching him how to read her. And when, finally, he realized what he should give, he knew even before he looked at the price that it would be the most expensive thing in the place.

The Book of Explorers

The "singing vine," so named by Ian Norcross following his first expedition to this region, does not, of course, sing. Typical whimsy on his part, that designation, and now we're stuck with it. The sound it produces when touched does not strike any of us as resembling a human singing voice. A reedy whistle, at best; an occasional atonal whine or cry.

We plod on. Kirby in the lead with his rusted machete, hacking away. Annoyingly, he seems to be invigorated by the humid stew we breathe instead of air. Great swinging arcs of the blade; lusty grunted exhalations. Tiny toneless shrieks from the scattered singing vines.

At a rough clearing of sorts—an area of moss, mushrooms, and rotted stumps—we set up camp for the night. Pamela stakes the tent. Kirby clears the perimeter, hoisting branches and rocks into the growing dark, expanding our territory. Wakefield attempts a fire. I remove provisions. Luntz, notepad out, sketches a plant sprouting from the cleft in a red stump. After dusk, from the Kirby-carved tunnel of forest, Esterling appears like a just-risen nocturnal creature, taking us all by surprise. We hadn't realized he had lagged so far behind.

Night in the tent: Luntz and Wakefield fetal, silent. Kirby heaving and grunting and making truncated machete-arm swings in his sleep, still at work, hacking his way through dreams. Pamela, I sense, is awake like me. Outside, the fire's still going. I can hear it pop, hear Esterling pacing. His shadow wavers across the tent wall, growing and shrinking and growing again. Pamela has chosen to place her sleeping bag beside mine, unnecessarily close, it seems to me. A testing closeness, as if to prove (to me? to herself?) that, as she has always maintained, we can work together professionally in spite of the divorce . . .

The next day Kirby is pierced by something. Thorn, insect tail, fang—we don't know. He hacks even faster than usual, as if fueled by it. We produce the kit. We propose antibiotic ointment, antivenom, water, bandages, rest. Kirby will have none of it. He hacks furiously away.

We set up camp at a rough clearing of sorts, an area of moss, mushrooms, rotted stumps. I collect soil samples. Pamela takes photographs. Kirby, cross-legged in the dirt, glares fiercely through smudged spectacles at the infection in his leg, at its purplish flowering core and the pus-green tendrils radiating outward across his calf. Luntz is sitting on a rock, speaking softly to a nearby singing vine. Only Esterling stands apart, at camp's edge, gazing into the forest. He seems never to have recovered from his year of solitary research at Lake Tanganyika. Try to talk to him and he looks back at you, face closed, vast watery distances in his eyes . . .

The next morning, Kirby refuses to come out of his sleeping bag. His voice sounds lucid enough, but he refuses to come out of his sleeping bag. He's sealed himself inside. He talks about the "risk of contagion," although it's unclear whether the contagion risk is to us or to himself. We stand above him. Our eyes meet: delirium. Whispered counsel at a jagged stump. Kirby hops from the tent, still sleeping-bagged, insisting in a hearty if muffled voice that he can go on . . .

Now I'm on hacking duty. Pamela's idea, basically. I'm the strongest, she says. None of the others—not even Wakefield, three inches taller than me and ten years younger—see the need to question that assertion. I'm assuming there will be a rotation. Atonal squeals shred and scatter around me.

I think of thorns, insect tails, fangs.

I think of Norcross. An entourage of locals to do *his* hacking. I picture him on a palanquin, body assuming a listless, reclining pose but face feverish under his pith helmet, glistening with exploratory greed . . . A notorious opium-eater, apparently, old Norcross. Until he discovered the *jijasa* root in this jungle. (Or, far more likely, it was introduced to him by the locals and he simply appropriated the credit.) A revision to the image, then: same listless recline, face still feverish, but ruminant as his jaws work the root, a brown leak of drool at mouth's edge . . .

Behind me, I hear a progressive crash through layers of vegetation. Kirby, hopping at the rear, has made another tunnel, this time with himself. The sleeping bag careens past vines, branches, undergrowth, a green shape hurtling through deeper green, toppling eventually into a stream, where it squirms, splashes, folds, shudders, stretches, twists, stops.

Why does it fall to me to unzip the bag? I choose what I suspect is the end with the head and open it slightly, tentatively, enough to see what needs to be seen.

Downstream we find a waterfall. A gentle push of collective hands sends the bag over the edge. Tears are shed and private items, separated from the useful ones in his gear, are tossed over the spray in an improvised eulogy. Pamela says something on behalf of us all, her words lost in the roaring hush of the water.

I'm glad we decided—*I* decided; it was my insistence—not to bring along Mabel. Five-year-olds should not be brought on jungle expeditions, no matter how preternaturally gifted. Anyway she has a presentation to give at a symposium on TMCDB&AG (Theoretical Molecular, Cellular, Developmental Bioengineering, and Applied Genetics) and would certainly have opposed the idea.

In our absence, she is being tended by what Pamela and I call the Gang of Nine: a retinue of research assistants, doctoral candidates, and veteran academics, hovering, fussing, fawning, and, I suspect, attempting surreptitiously to draw from her material for future books and articles. With them she acts two years younger than her age. Alarmingly imperious, she issues more or less arbitrary commands in a cloying species of baby talk she never used when she was actually a baby. As far as I know, she never gives them what they want. They are frustrated even as they are smitten with surrogate parental devotion, which frustrates them even more.

How did we produce her? We, who are nothing but explorers. You could call it miraculous. You could just as well call it freakish. Frightening. Our offspring: off of us—off of Pamela—she sprang. My contribution a full 50 percent only in the genetic sense. Otherwise peripheral, however much I've tried to make up for that since. To make up for not having grown her inside me, for not having been the one to deliver her from womb to world. Waiting instead on the sidelines for my chance to be useful.

We fail to find a decent clearing: no moss, no mushrooms, no rotted stumps. Pamela blames me in my capacity as machete wielder. We settle instead for an abbreviated glade.

Before the marriage, in our trysts, our assignations, our impulsive couplings, our flash fucks, Pamela and I chose natural settings: parks, wooded glens, semi-secluded folds of land.

We had cause then to be secretive, yet we chose green public places. I remember we did it in high grass a lot. This in spite of insects, pebbles, thistles, branches, assorted litter . . . Things poked at us, swarmed us, rubbed us raw, and we didn't care. Then we got married and became explorers . . .

Night in the tent. Even Esterling has retired to his sleeping bag. He sleeps rigid, silent. The entire tent is silent. No heaving, no grunting. No truncated swings. Am I the only one awake?

Luntz makes a discovery halfway through the next day's trek. He's found the *jijasa* root; or believes he has. We set up camp for the night near a brook, the sound of a waterfall somewhere above. After dinner I hack the root into equal portions. We chew in a circle around the fire and imagine ourselves—or I imagine myself—in an ancient ritual, a link to something primeval. The root tastes primeval, anyway. We wait—I wait—for a vision . . . On the other side of the fire, Wakefield and Pamela are doing things I prefer not to see . . . I wander off by myself, away from the camp.

"We should go back," Esterling says to me. He appears to have been standing next to me. Back where? To the fire?

"We don't belong here. Not anymore." I can't remember the last time he said something. Days, maybe. Days of silence, and when he chooses to speak, it's to utter ominous words after I've chewed a psychotropic root. Aside from the fact that he's talking, he seems unchanged by the plant, as grimly affectless as ever. I agree with him, for something to say. The forest makes its forest noises, only somehow more deeply, more three-dimensionally. Wakefield and Pamela: I didn't see it coming . . .

I look around: Esterling is gone. Through the black cage of branches, the fire, very distant, mechanical in its glow, its crackle and sputter. It's like one of those fake, glowing yule-tide logs, pulsed in apparently random patterns by some hidden circuit. Made to seem natural. Only the fire is not distant. I'm sitting right in front of it. Eager noises from the tent, one of them familiar, belonging to Pamela. It occurs to me that the mosquitoes swarming me are not just hungry on their own; they are the emissaries, the mouths of a hunger out there beyond the yuletide fire. This is not a terrifying thought. Why shouldn't I be food? I watch the mosquitoes work. It's a kind of communion. An offering. Wakefield meanders past, unclothed, dragging a burnt stick. More food for the hunger out there. But then, in that case, if he's here, what about the noises coming from the tent? I remain outside, watching the zipped flap. I must have failed at some point in my vigil, though: in the morning I find myself on my side in a pile of bark chips, the base of the tree trunk beside me denuded in a perfectly even ring.

No sign today, in anyone's behavior, of last night's excesses, of unmentionable tented debaucheries. All of us are absent-minded and irritable, all of us except for Esterling. He emerges, surprisingly, as the leader. For the moment at least. Not that he issues orders or even speaks, but his no-nonsense consumption of breakfast and matter-of-fact packing put us on notice and get us moving too.

My mind keeps returning to the tent. "About last night," I say to Pamela, pausing beside her as she zips her pack. "You don't have to apologize, Daniel," she says. "You weren't your-self." She tugs at my arm. I realize that it's the machete arm. She gives me a gentle push forward, toward the wall of vegetation.

Hacking, hacking. Thorns, tails, fangs . . . I think of Mabel, orphaned. Of all the things I still had to learn from her. Lessons on the plaid couch that will never take place again. Mabel propped in a corner, primly professorial, small hands at the knobs of the Etch A Sketch she uses as her blackboard . . .

I realize that no one is behind me. I return through the tunnel I've carved to find Wakefield, Luntz, and Pamela stopped, faces uptilted, staring at something in the trees. A green sleeping bag, Kirby's from the look of it. It hangs full above us, a torn end snagged on a cluster of drooping branches, swaying slightly. After a while Esterling marches by, oblivious, as if he doesn't see anything unusual dangling overhead, as if we're hallucinating it . . .

Back into the tunnel. Hacking. Hiking. Collected soil samples. Camp. Sleep (fitful). Repacked packs.

Nobody has mentioned Kirby's sleeping bag.

Am I the group's leader now? It's a question I ask myself again and again as the days pass. If Kirby, carving away at the front of the line, was leading our expedition, that should make me the leader now. I don't feel like the leader. But if I am, where am I leading us?

Overheard while collecting soil samples:

Wakefield: "Well but it's not a question of faith, is it? It's a question of what can actually be accomplished."

Pamela: "Tell *him* that."

Hacking, hacking: the forest is a membrane, reluctantly yielding, resisting our advance. There is always more forest. An occasional cavity, a pocket with mushrooms and rotted stumps, then more forest. Years of exploring, and this is what I've learned: there's always more . . .

I make a decision. I turn to the others, shuffling along in my wake, and, proffering the machete, suggest a rotation. A changing of the guard. Wakefield interests himself in a trans-lucent egg sac blobbed on a nearby leaf. Pamela fiddles with equipment, untangling cords, turning dials. Luntz has pro-duced his notepad; lifting a pencil, he puts a fingertip to its pointed end. Esterling, trailing somewhere behind, a caboose unlinked from the train, would probably take the machete if I offered it to him, but do I really want to place a large, sharp-ened blade in his care?

Esterling's year alone at Lake Tanganyika: it's difficult to imagine. I've never been on an expedition without Pamela. He returned and promptly published a series of papers describing what he'd learned: the "diplomatic protocols" in territorial dis-putes between neighboring species of African ants; a hitherto unknown stage in the life cycle of the aphid; the parthenoge-netic mating patterns of the Tanganyikan humphead, the only cichlid—Esterling discovered—capable of asexual reproduc-tion. He spent months observing algae. In his final published paper he claimed that algae distribution patterns on subsurface mineral shelves constituted a "holographic representation" of the health of the lake's larger ecosystem . . .

Unpublished, unrevealed: whatever it was in his solitary research that changed him.

Or was it the solitude itself? Just Esterling and a lake. I can't imagine being alone like that. Yet . . . A life alone, without Pamela: Isn't that what I have now, even if we *are* still exploring together?

Together and not together.

Midmorning. Rain comes without warning, sunlight still in tatters all around, then continues all day unabated. Behind me I can hear Luntz whistling tonelessly. The hacking is slow and sprays wet now as well as vines. When the rain stops, it's also without warning, a faucet that's been turned off. Some species of leech (we think) has secured itself to Wakefield's forehead. We attempt to peel it away. It declines. We pull, pry, salt, and slather it, trying to urge it off. It holds fast to the unlined skin, curved there quizzically like a third eyebrow with no eye beneath it . . .

More forest. Always more forest.

I gave Mabel a book when she was little. Littler, I mean, than she is now. It's called *The Book of Explorers*. One glossy page shows a painting of a grizzled mapmaker. The picture captures him just as he's finished pushing his way through a thicket, into the open. He's at a cliff's edge. And before him—he stands agape—are vistas, tier upon tier, a sudden and unexpected richness of view, rumpled and multicolored and apparently endless . . .

I approach Pamela. I want to talk. About the *jijasa* night, about Kirby's sleeping bag, about the expedition's growing loss of focus. About Mabel. "You can see that now is not the time," she says. "I'm examining the flauna." Pamela uses this word. Flauna. She uses it to mean the interrelationship, the symbiosis of flora and fauna. She uses the word in public. At dinner parties, at lectures. I've talked to her about it. She won't stop.

"Besides," she says, "don't you have soil samples to collect?"

"Pamela," I say.

"Onward, Roald." She points away into the forest. She calls me Roald sometimes. After Roald Amundsen, the first explorer to reach the South Pole. A hero of mine, for some reason that I can no longer remember. Something other than being the first, surely. Surely I had something better in mind than making a hero of someone simply because he got there first. I don't remember. Roald: it was an endearment, used by Pamela in those moments—more and more infrequent near the end—

when irony and genuine feeling were able to coexist. I'm not sure it sounds like an endearment now . . .

If I could have spawned Mabel myself, parthenogenetically, no need for Pamela, my gifted daughter springing off me like Athena from the split in Zeus's skull . . .

It rains and it stops. Faucet on, faucet off.

Wakefield's new eyebrow, still curved quizzically, fattens on his forehead.

I have many soil samples now. I keep them in a sealed case, in labeled vials that fit perfectly into the molded plastic. When the last soil-filled vial is fit into place, I will be finished collecting samples. I don't know the purpose of these samples. It's not necessary to know, I've been told. Something will be done with them. For professional explorers like Pamela and myself, there are things you concern yourself with and things you don't let yourself worry about. "Above our pay grade, Daniel," Pamela says. Or said, in the old days. In a funny, gruff voice. Making fun of our willed ignorance, making fun of our making fun of it . . .

When I first read *The Book of Explorers* to Mabel, I tried to explain the joy of exploring for its own sake. I'm not sure I was convincing. I'm not sure I was convinced myself. Mabel wasn't interested. She didn't care about these men (in the book, it's all men) and their achievements . . . Basically, Mabel just isn't interested in explorers. In exploration. It bores her. Mabel is interested, I guess, in mental exploration.

She—to the extent I can understand her complex thinking and her still-limited English—is of the opinion that Nature is not a collection or even interconnection of *things*, nor even a process, in the Darwinian sense, but—if I'm getting her right—a system of messages that reveals itself in the thingness we call Nature. But—and I know this is probably beside the point—messages sent by whom, and to whom? It's a question I can't ask her. There would be the pursed lips, the sad and embarrassed sideward glance . . .

Stepping out of the tunnel and into a clearing, we all observe it: the blackened remains of a campfire, near a brook. We pitch the tent and set out supplies, working around the remains, not looking at them or at each other. Then scatter, each to his or her business. A distant roar of water somewhere above. At the edge of the clearing I come across the entrance to another tunnel, recently carved, not yet completely covered over with new forest. I push my way inside. It's still possible, if only barely, to make it through without the machete. After a minute or two of pushing I practically run into Pamela, standing in speckled shadow, recording equipment Velcroed to her vest and cradled in her hands. She's looking up, at Kirby's sleeping bag. I stop beside her and look up too. The bag turns, very slowly, beneath its cluster of branches. Pamela is perfectly still; she has her recording equipment ready, but I can see she hasn't turned it on; or she's already turned it off. We stand there, looking up. It's the first time during the whole expedition, I realize, that Pamela and I have been alone together without her sending me away. The bag turns. As we watch, there is, from time to time, or there seems to be, movement from within—a shifting, a rounded bulging, a subtle changing of shape . . .

Now, as our expedition moves through the forest, in our zigzagging lines or arcs or possibly only in circles, I keep imagining myself coming upon Kirby's sleeping bag again. Only this time nearly tripping on it where it lies below me, a green heap, unzipped, flung open. Discarded . . .

It is a historical fact that Roald Amundsen never returned

from his final expedition. It is also a fact that his body was never found. Another explorer lost searching for lost explorers. The Heroic Age of Antarctic Exploration: that's the accepted name for Amundsen's era. And the present age? Would it merit that kind of fearless capitalization? Would it merit a name at all?

My hacking—there has been no rotation; there will never be a rotation—ends abruptly in a patch of sand. I step into unreasonable brightness. No vistas, no tier upon tier of rich view, but space at least, open space and, in the distance, broken purple shapes. We've reached the "Sandbox," as it's called, the name another gift from Norcross. Not completely inaccurate, in this case: a terrain of gold dunes, a microdesert roughly three miles square. It's not bad, for a desert. Hot, obviously. But freedom from the humidity seems like a blessing for the first quarter mile or so. We stay in line, for some reason. Me at the head. Machete at my belt. Luntz stops once, to kneel before the desert's single cactus.

We near the purple shapes. The "Plush Mountains." (Blame Norcross.)

We pause at the base. Nobody's inclined to approach. The Plush Mountains. Not mountains, really: piled and shattered surfaces; ridges and cliffs and canyons. The velvety material lining the rocks, Luntz speculates aloud, is most likely some type of lichen. Although possibly a bryophyte. He stands there beside us, speculating from a distance, as if reluctant to touch the plush.

Wakefield makes a surprised sound, a strangled half-word stuck in his throat. The beginning of "yesterday," it sounds like. He's looking through his binoculars, eyebrows above them curved now as quizzically as his third eyebrow. It's Esterling. He's climbing the plush, a crablike scaling, small, already far above. We call to him, we send up cheers and warnings, knowing we'll be ignored.

Norcross's memoir recounts his discovery of a "naturally formed staircase" at the base of these "mountains." We walk back and forth—sheer faces everywhere—until we think we've found it. Although, if we have, "staircase" is a generous description. Anyway a vaguely steplike upward succession of rocks, highly uneven but probably climbable. I clamber up the first step. The plush is soft, pleasant to touch, as velvety as it looks.

I think of Norcross climbing . . . These same "stairs"? Climbing and chewing *jijasa* root. At the top, if his at times hyperbolic memoir is to be believed, there should be a "naturally formed archway," followed by a large level area. The site of Norcross's famous root-induced vision: carved into the rock there his own face, enormous, covered in plush . . .

I look down: the Sandbox's gold square. Then the forest, no sign of our progress through it, no path visible, the trail I carved hidden beneath the canopy. Steam billows ceaselessly from the treetops like the smoke from a thousand chimneys. Beyond the forest there is, there should be, ocean—our starting point. You can make out a blue line far away, but can't tell if it's ocean or a strip of sky between steam and cloud. I want to identify it as ocean so that I can look back at where we started, see how far we've come . . .

Above: what can, in all fairness to Norcross, only be described as a naturally formed archway.

We pass beneath it, entering a large level area. Exhausted, we collapse onto the plush . . . I half expect to see Norcross's face in stone, his vision made real. Or our own faces, waiting for us. But there's nothing like that. No plush-covered Pamela. No Wakefield, no Luntz. My own face, nowhere to be seen . . . Only rocks and more rocks. The terrain is not inviting. It's not rejecting either. The terrain is not expressing an opinion regarding our presence there one way or the other. What would Kirby think? Maybe the view, the terrain— maybe it's all more interesting from a higher vantage point. Maybe Esterling has crab-crawled his way above us to something better.

It occurs to me that Mabel will be delivering her presentation at the symposium soon. Or already has. I've lost track of the date. I should probably have been there to hear her speak. Pamela and I both. Over my head, probably, but still. When she speaks before groups she sways. She links first finger with first finger and swings the link in front of her. Her good-luck charm, or a talisman to ward off frivolous and irrelevant questions from the audience. She's prone to error when using comparative adjectives, a rare lapse. "Because this is a more bigger problem," she might say. Her audience will be forgiving. She's five years old. They're there for her ideas, after all. Although her theory, I suspect, still needs work. It's still in its early stages. I should be there to hear it. I would try my best to understand. I want to understand. At the same time, it scares me. I don't know where Pamela and I fit into it. If there's room for people like us.

In *The Book of Explorers* there's a photograph of Roald Amundsen, taken shortly before his disappearance. The scene is desolate. He stands leaning in skis, alone in the center of the frame. The ridiculous, oversized, heroic mustache that accompanied him on earlier expeditions is gone. This is late Amundsen, shorn of twinkling eyes and dashing whiskers, Amundsen the stoical grand old man of exploration. Beside him, a sled loaded with supplies. The only way to tell that he's reached his goal is the flagpole thrust aslant in the snow. Amundsen's mitten grips it; his face, within his hood's ring of fur, is small, pinched, masklike. He grips the pole as if he would otherwise be blown away, leaning in his skis. White all around.

Kurobe and the Secrets

of Puppetry

Following his final performance before the Emperor, Choemon Kurobe—seventh-generation Master Puppeteer, three-time invitee to the private stage of the Tokugawa shogunate, imperially designated Living Artistic Treasure—was given a fish. His impending retirement had become common knowledge. Since there was, however, as yet no formal announcement, a grand and ostentatious parting gift (a summer home in Kyoto? a gilded statue of a puppet?) in the end hardly seemed appropriate. Gift after gift was considered and rejected before His Imperial Majesty learned of the old master's devotion to his carp pond.

The chosen fish was silver-blue in color and nearly three hands in length. The line had been bred over generations by the Imperial Fishkeeper to enrich the patterning and deepen the hue. The very existence of such a fish was unknown beyond the palace gates. Master Kurobe was of course present to witness the introduction of the remarkable gift into his pond. It nosed the surface dubiously, traced a wavering ellipse, and darted under the bridge. The next day Kurobe returned. On the third day, after gazing for a long time at the fish as it traveled through the green water, he decided that there was something wrong with it.

For years Kurobe had been in the habit of visiting his pond when contemplating a problem. The orderly movement of his carp as they made their slow circuits always calmed his mind. More than once he had found precisely the answer he'd been seeking there at the pond's edge. But on this day, the longer he remained, the more troubled he became: the Emperor's fish, he'd discovered, had the oddest tendency to change direction as if it had lost its bearings; it flailed at its pondmates with nervous swipes of its speckled tail; it flipped and twisted, trapped in an imaginary net. Its senseless movements were unnerving. As he watched, the creature scraped the pool's bottom and vanished in a muddy plume of disturbed water; and it seemed to Kurobe that it was not the pool but his own thoughts that were being clouded over . . .

The problem he had come here hoping to solve concerned the naming of a successor: for months now he had vacillated, unable to choose between his sons. Each had his strengths. And yet . . . He recalled something he had been fond of telling his wife: "If we could just find a way to squeeze those two into one," he would say, "they might make a fine man." His wife would frown and slap at his arm, feigning disapproval. She knew, after all, that it was only a joke—barbed perhaps, but spoken with affection.

As assistants, his sons were all he could ask for: Master Kurobe operated the puppet's right hand as well as the stick and levers animating its head; Genzo, the elder, controlled the left hand; Sojiro its feet. Kurobe was the star, of course, resplendent in his gold performing kimono as he displayed the miracle of his technique. Audiences came to see him more even than the figures he led across the stage; or, rather, they came to see them together, master and puppet, the creator present in his own creation. The same could not be said for Kurobe's sons: like all assistants, they were, by accepted convention, forgotten, the audience politely disregarding their presence as they followed behind their father in black hooded robes like shadows cast in opposite directions. But when Kurobe left the stage for the final time, one of them would have to remove the hood and step forward as lead puppeteer, and Kurobe could not imagine either filling the role.

Twilight had darkened the pond; the fish were only moving glints of color. Bats veered and tumbled overhead. He started back along the path; but dusk's inscrutable melancholy had filled the garden, and he found himself lingering. The cypress: it needed pruning. He would have to tell the gardener. He stopped beneath his favorite, an old persimmon whose blossoms had finished falling a week before. He could make out a few, shriveled and brown, in the grass at his feet.

His fingertips found the juncture of trunk and limb; felt a branch's rough curve; crossed a nub where a cut had healed. He was, at first, thinking about sons and succession. Then . . .

Then it was dark. There he was, standing in darkness. Night had whirred softly to life around him. And his fingers, he discovered, were still rasping blindly over the bark of his persimmon tree . . .

In the common room, Genzo was stretched out beside his usual bottle of sake.

"Father!" he cried as Kurobe passed, waving him inside.

"Wait till you hear what I saw in the quarter last night!"

His son's enthusiasm made Kurobe feel suddenly weary.

"I was wandering down this side street, right? Near The

Dancing Fox, which used to be a— Anyway, I saw some people gathered around, laughing and, you know, making a general commotion. A bunch of drunks. So I go up to have a look, and it turns out they're watching this busker. But not your usual clown or juggler. This fellow, he's doing a sort of . . . burlesque of puppet theater, I guess you'd call it. Jerking around like a puppet, playing every part, male and female, changing wigs and costumes in a flash. And all the while providing his own narration. Pretty soon I was laughing like the rest of them, I couldn't help it, I mean he *was* hilarious, Father. Honestly. But very skilled too. Not just some fool. At one point, there was something he did, I . . . I thought I saw a sort of . . . Well, never mind. Anyway, you want to know the best part? He barely came up to here!" His hand sliced a thigh. "Easily the smallest man I've ever seen! See, that was the hook: he wasn't just playing the part of a puppet, he was the size of one himself!"

Kurobe said nothing. His son was well aware of how he felt about performers attempting parts intended for the puppet theater.

Actors, of course, had always been whores, showcasing their charms onstage to entice customers into later offstage adventures. Kurobe had no particular quarrel with this; let them do as they liked in their own sordid world. But to attempt the plays of Chikamatsu! It was this belated claim to respectability that Kurobe found intolerable. Their recent artistic pretensions; their posturing and bombast as they blundered through ludicrous impersonations of puppetry's greatest heroes . . . Kurobe even had it on good authority that a popular Kabuki actor was openly stealing from one of Kurobe's most celebrated characterizations, imitating his puppet down to the last gesture. Of course, sophisticated audiences understood that, in the hands of a master, a puppet came more vividly to life onstage than any human counterpart. But the rabble couldn't be expected to appreciate the difference; they were eating up these Kabuki charades. It was shameful, all of it. Far more shameful than whatever the actors got up to in their private rooms after their shows . . . But wait: he'd lost his train of . . . Actors? No; his son had been raving about something. Worse than an actor: a beggar, that was it. A deformed beggar making a deliberate mockery of Kurobe's art for a laugh and a handful of tossed coins . . .

Was Genzo trying to provoke him? Kurobe hadn't spoken to his sons yet of his plan to retire, but it had become an open secret; and Genzo was behaving even worse than usual these days, as if determined to undermine his own chances of succession.

". . . So I thought," his son was saying, "maybe we could go to the quarter together and see him. I'm telling you, Father, you really would be surprised. We could stop along the way, have a drink . . ."

"You know perfectly well that's not the sort of place where I choose to spend my time," Kurobe said in his most dignified tone.

For an instant Genzo winced as though struck, causing Kurobe to wonder if the invitation he'd taken as a taunt might have been sincere after all; but then a crooked smirk distorted half of his son's face. It was an expression Kurobe was all too familiar with: ever since childhood, when confronted with his father's anger, it would appear, a lopsided look of satisfaction, as if he weren't being scolded at all but rather praised instead.

"I'm sure it's a fine sight you make: a Kurobe, wandering the quarter every night like a stray dog sniffing for scraps."

"Right. That's a 'no' then, I take it." Even the smirk had gone; now Genzo merely looked bored.

"You've no self-respect, that's clear enough; but you might at least try to consider your family name." He was tired. His words felt tired, a script repeated too many times. A script to a play with no ending. Did he still believe his own words? He had once, perhaps; but even his disappointment in his son seemed like something he'd given up on long before.

"Finished already?" Genzo poured himself more sake. "You forgot the part about how ashamed Mother would be if she were alive to see me now . . ." And he let his head loll to one side as if to appear drunker than he really was.

At the sudden mention of his wife, Kurobe found himself unable to speak. Even now. How dare he speak of her. Dazed, he stumbled toward the doorway as if through a darkened corridor.

"Well, good night to you too!" his son sang out.

For him nothing.

It wasn't just spite: who had earned his title if not Sojiro? Reward filial piety; reward duty. Yes: as he should have done all along. But by the time he reached his room, his resolve had already vanished, and he felt even more uncertain than before, as if each attempt at a decision only drained a bit more of his will to actually decide.

His daughter-in-law had unrolled his futon for him, lit the lamp, and set on a table the glass of wheat tea he liked before bed. He began to undress. If those two could just squeeze into one. His wife's frown; her light slap. They might make a fine man. It had seemed a joke, nothing more . . .

The trouble with Genzo was obvious enough, not only to Kurobe, but probably to everyone in the city: his nightly carousing, his gambling, his disdain for all that was proper in an elder son. When he *was* at home he could usually be found sprawled across a mat, claiming to be dreaming up a fantastic new puppet drama which somehow never reached completion. Tradition dictated that Kurobe's title pass to him; but it was a part for which he was disastrously miscast. Kurobe could no longer blame his son's waywardness on his age: he wasn't so young anymore. And still he refused to marry. With Genzo as Master Puppeteer, Kurobe could see already how it would be: onstage he would shine brilliantly; then, afterward, he would resume his real work, the only work to which he had ever been truly committed: ruining himself and his family name. Kurobe had detected this in him from the earliest age. Genzo had the preternatural ability to gift puppets with life even before learning the skills which should have made such a thing possible; but only if he saw it as a game, a form of play. Whenever discipline was required his son would turn limp, his eyes would go dark, and Kurobe could feel the boy slide away even as he remained there unmoving beside him . . .

The trouble with his younger son was quite a different matter altogether, and certainly not something he could have explained properly to anyone who might have asked. Violating the rule of succession did not in itself especially bother Kurobe; exceptions, after all, were hardly unknown. Not every eldest son was fit to carry on his father's work. No; the trouble was Sojiro himself. As a child, he had been a fine apprentice. He soon surpassed his daydreaming brother in all the essentials of puppeteering, and by thirteen had learned every drama in his father's repertoire. It wasn't only puppetry, though; he brought to any task the same sober resolve. If Kurobe had been a mat-maker his son would have shown exactly the same dedication. Kurobe knew he should have been proud. Yet at times his son's devotion to duty had unnerved him, as if Sojiro were not really a child at all but an adult in disguise. Adulthood, predictably, brought few changes; he grew perhaps more severe. He had by that time systematically mastered all he'd been taught. In his dependable hands the puppets reproduced the subtlest gestures, the most intricate movements of the human form; but they never breathed. The worst part was that his son seemed unable to sense anything missing. He didn't grasp that it was possible or even desirable for the puppet to be more than a collection of parts held together by rope and thread. He couldn't be blamed; it wasn't a failing, but rather a lack. It was Kurobe who had failed: he had transmitted to his son everything except what mattered most. But the question remained: how could Kurobe bequeath his legacy to a . . . technician? Choosing Sojiro, he feared, meant dooming his descendants to mediocrity, to a gradual watering down of the Kurobe blood, until nothing but skill remained. A family of artists, reduced to a family of competent artisans. And even that fate in doubt: his daughter-in-law seemed barren; after seven years of marriage she had yet to give him a single grandchild.

When no fitting successor emerged within a family, there was one other possibility: the master could adopt an apprentice, awarding him name and title. Here at least the heritage of artistic excellence could be preserved, even if the bloodline was severed. Kurobe's theater had its share of fine puppeteers, but they had all apprenticed elsewhere; his only apprentices were his sons. And it was too late now to start anew: twenty years would be required for even the most talented student to master the intricacies of his art; and Kurobe had no more time.

No more time: for months now he had been noticing the change in himself; and although it had so far manifested in only the mildest of ways, he recognized that he was suffering from more than the ordinary absentmindedness of old age. At times he would feel something open in him; something would yawn and wait, expectant . . . And then he would recover, wondering how much time had passed and whether anyone had noticed. Until now he had been able to conceal his condition. His greatest fear, though, was that it would one day strike during a performance. He knew what was in store for him, or imagined that he did. And he told himself he was ready to face it. He wasn't afraid. What he could not face, though, what he found absolutely insupportable, was the possibility of the illness touching his puppetry. This—the thought of contamination and decay seeping into the art he'd spent a lifetime striving to purify—this was what made his fingertips turn numb and his heart freeze in his chest . . .

He finished his tea and allowed himself to lie down. Just for a moment. It was too early for bed; there was still rehearsing to do.

He thought of his father. He had been a gentle man, but also somehow intimidating, perhaps because he rarely spoke. Even the skills of puppetry had—to the best of Kurobe's recollection—been taught mostly by example. As a child, Kurobe's days were spent at the theater, watching his father rehearse. The way he changed onstage! Glaring as fiercely as the warrior puppets he specialized in controlling. And always in his flashing gold kimono crested with plum blossoms, the same kimono Kurobe had worn while performing for how many years now . . . ? He was too drowsy to count . . . What had he been thinking about? His father: the theater. The only time he stopped rehearsing was during New Year's celebrations. They would go kite-flying then, just the two of them, if the weather was right . . . Above him, the paper rectangle would swerve in the cold blue. He could hear its distant rustle and snap, feel it tug and shift, trying to pull free of his grasp. His father steadied his hand . . .

He dreamed that they crouched together on what seemed a mound or nest of mud and twigs, holding a line. Others, whose faces he couldn't make out, stood knee-deep in the water. Kurobe understood that they had gathered to watch. He and his father held the line, but the fish yanked madly, thrashing through the reeds; and Kurobe was terrified because he knew that at any moment the line was bound to break and the fish would vanish into the mottled marshwater, the hook still buried deep in its mouth . . .

❀   ❀   ❀

The next day Genzo brought home a visitor. Smiling mysteriously, he announced the arrival of a distinguished guest, then vanished before Kurobe could ask for the guest's name. Feeling flustered and irritable, Kurobe hurried into his finest clothes, ordered his daughter-in-law to prepare tea and sweets, then slid open the door of the visitors' room to find his son seated beside a figure the size of a large doll. The figure gave off so many contradictory impressions that it was necessary to take it in gradually, in stages: it wore what seemed at first glance an elegant gentleman's kimono, but closer inspection revealed a crudely sewn stage costume of poor material, faded and fraying in places; the shrunken head might have been an old man's, with its sparse hair and puckered skin; yet its posture, as it sat there formally, legs folded beneath it, was erect and gave an impression of youthful vigor; and the eyes, in their deep folds of flesh, seemed as bright and guileless as a child's.

He realized at once that this must be the street performer Genzo had spoken of, but his sense of decorum prevented him from scolding his son in front of a guest, even this one. He sat down, ignoring Genzo's smirk, and greeted the creature with a bow. It bowed in return, so deeply that its forehead nearly struck the mat.

"My name is Oike," it said in a high, strangled voice. "It's a great honor to meet you, sir. Thank you for your generous hospitality. Please allow me to apologize for the intrusion. It was terribly impolite of me."

"Not at all. Make yourself comfortable," Kurobe said, relieved and at the same time taken aback by the tiny figure's understanding of etiquette. He had imagined a creature incapable of ordinary speech, with the manners of a monkey. He wondered if his son had coached the busker before bringing him here.

The tea and sweets were brought in. Trembling, the creature bowed low again and begged the family's forgiveness, like a starving man being offered a feast; then sat very still, refusing even to sip his tea until Kurobe had taken a drink first.

"I struck up a conversation last night with Oike here," said Genzo, "and once he heard who I was, he went on and on about you, Father. He's a great admirer of your work."

Did Genzo really think he could be taken in by such transparent flattery? He turned indignantly from his son to the ragged creature his son had dared to invite into their home.

"I understand," he said, "that you perform an, ah—how shall I put it?—*appreciation* of puppet theater."

"Thank you for your choice of words, sir, but I'm afraid it's hardly an appreciation," the little man replied, his shriveled face reddening. "More of a travesty, really. It's not easy for someone like me to make a living, and this show of mine . . . Well, it at least allows me to get by. Although that's hardly an excuse for what I do. Still, it's true that my act, such as it is, was inspired by a genuine appreciation of your great art."

"His knowledge," Genzo said, popping a last bite of cake into his mouth, "is really quite extraordinary, Father. Greater than mine, I'd wager! From what I can tell"—he chewed, swallowed—"he knows your whole repertoire."

"Is that so? You've seen me perform, then?" It was unlikely that this creature would ever have been allowed into his theater.

"Only once, sir. As a boy. But my love of puppetry—I trace it all back to that experience. Since then I've had to rely on secondhand accounts of your performances. Your son is very kind; but the fact is, I know next to nothing, I'm afraid."

"Nonsense," said Genzo. "No need for false modesty here, Oike."

Kurobe might have suspected again that his son had simply coached Oike to win him over, except for the embarrassed yet earnest look on the little man's face. He found himself curious to know what Oike could possibly understand about his art. To test his knowledge, though, would be to act as a rude host; and even pursuing a conversation about Kurobe's own performances risked appearing immodest. Yet what else was there to say to this strange creature? He faltered, and the silence lengthened; finally his son, who appeared to be enjoying Kurobe's predicament immensely, said:

"He's especially fond of *Shogen's House*, Father. He went on and on about your interpretation."

Shogen's House was in fact the drama of which Kurobe was the most proud. Something in the story of Matahei, the stuttering artist denied his master's professional name because of his affliction, had always touched Kurobe more than any drama in puppet theater, and he had devoted much of his career to refining and deepening his characterization until he felt finally it could probably not be improved upon. In spite of himself, Kurobe said: "And what is it, if I may ask, that you found so remarkable about my interpretation? There's nothing special about it, I assure you."

The little man's eyes grew even brighter than before. "As I remember it—you'll have to forgive me, I shouldn't say anything, it was so long ago, I'm sure I'm not doing it justice, but, well, it seemed to me that the greatness—it's so many little things, isn't it? Details. But not details at all; not really. For instance, after Matahei decides to kill himself—I've never forgotten this—he's facing the fountain. And you . . . I can't describe it, the way you . . ."

Oike suddenly rose and began moving dreamily across the mat, seeming to forget where he was. It occurred to Kurobe that Oike was enacting the scene himself. His arm lifted, an imaginary brush in his hand; and as he gazed down at what Kurobe knew must be the stone fountain on which Matahei was about to paint his final self-portrait, Oike's face underwent a change. It became . . . another face. He stood there, poised, brush held aloft, the artist on the verge of creation . . . Then he came to himself, sat down, and resumed speaking, as if nothing had happened.

It had been the briefest sketch, used merely to illustrate Oike's point; but Kurobe was left with the odd sense that he had just watched his own puppet, or rather, everything he wished might appear in its painted face if it could magically soften into human expression. Kurobe had done everything in his power to make Matahei live onstage, and there were moments when the puppet had seemed almost to move of its own volition, moments when he was able to believe he had managed to incarnate Matahei in the figure he held; but Oike's performance made Kurobe feel keenly the limitations of wood and cloth, sticks and levers. Or perhaps it was Kurobe's own limitations as an artist . . . It seemed to him that he had finally been given a glimpse of the true Matahei, his beloved puppet nothing more than a makeshift surrogate.

Kurobe and Oike talked all afternoon. Oike possessed an impressive grasp of the essentials of puppetry, just as Genzo had claimed; and though his knowledge was incomplete and marred by occasional error, this seemed the unavoidable result of studying an art secondhand. Kurobe was tempted to correct, to clarify, to share his insights and expertise, but held himself in check—he wasn't about to let his son feel he'd been won over so easily; besides, he was afraid to sound like some blustering old fool. Still, he felt he had perhaps never spoken to someone with a greater love of his art. When Oike rose to leave, Kurobe—to Genzo's obvious surprise—invited him to come again.

Afterward, Kurobe couldn't forget the moment when Oike became Matahei. A face kept appearing before him: it hung suspended there, the face of the artist, still a puppet but human now as well, its shrunken face seeming to gaze back at him in some sort of mysterious reproach. The next night, for the first time in many years, he went to the pleasure quarter. He was soon lost in a tangle of dark streets. It was too hot to be out walking; before long his summer kimono was soaked. He kept searching. He remembered his son mentioning a Dancing Fox, and began asking until he finally came upon a second-rate geisha house by that name. But there were no buskers in sight. He only found Oike by chance. He had given up, and was making his way home when he noticed a crowd gathered around a doorway lit faintly by a candle in the window above. They were looking down at their feet and laughing raucously as if at the antics of a trained animal. As Kurobe approached, Oike came into view, dressed in a noblewoman's kimono and ornamented wig that looked as if they had been designed for a child. Kurobe concealed himself as best he could behind the others and watched.

He had hoped to see in the performance something of what he had glimpsed at his home the day before; but Oike's act was such pure buffoonery that he began to doubt he had glimpsed it at all. Where before he had seemed to bring a puppet to life, now Oike appeared determined to ruthlessly eradicate all that was human in him, until only an animated but lifeless figure remained to prance mechanically over the cobblestones. If anything, he moved with less grace than a puppet, deliberately exaggerating for comedic effect all of the limits imposed by the techniques of puppeteering. It was impossible to believe that this was the same man who had spoken so fervently the day before about Kurobe's art. There were, admittedly, moments of sly wit intended for those who might know a thing or two about puppet theater; but for the most part it was all base nonsense. Yet he could not even feel offended by what he saw—Oike was, in the end, ridiculing himself and his deformity at least as much as he was ridiculing the art of puppetry.

Kurobe stepped further into the shadows. He feared being recognized. Yet he was unable to leave. The tiny figure cavorted under the candlelight while Kurobe watched, held in place by horror, and as he watched, he found himself more and more ashamed, as if it were he and not Oike who was to blame for this sad spectacle . . .

The next time Oike visited, Kurobe mentioned nothing of what he had seen. They talked again for hours, about puppetry, mostly, although the little man displayed a surprising knowledge of other performing arts, including even sleight of hand—at Kurobe's insistence, he performed a simple yet baffling trick with an inverted cup and a crumpled piece of paper. At one point, in the middle of a conversation about Chikamatsu's greatest plays, Kurobe was astonished to find that he couldn't recall the name of the courtesan from *The Uprooted Pine*. He froze, concentrating. After a discreet pause Oike said, "Azuma," in almost a whisper, pronouncing the name like an incantation, and it was as though Kurobe's own memory had whispered to him the word he'd been searching for.

When evening came, Kurobe had his daughter-in-law set an extra place for dinner. Genzo was nowhere to be seen; but Sojiro arrived punctually, as always. He stopped in the doorway. Finding himself oddly defensive, Kurobe began explaining, in perhaps more detail than was necessary, who Oike was and how he'd come to be there. His son was civil but even quieter than usual during the meal, and the oppressive feeling didn't leave Kurobe until he and the little man were out of the house and strolling together through the garden.

"Forgive me for prying, but how is it that you came to perform on the street?" Kurobe asked.

There was a splash from the pool. A carp had risen, silvery, to the surface. It gulped air, shivered once like a ripple of reflected moon, and sank again into the black water. The Emperor's mad fish, Kurobe thought uneasily.

"I'm afraid it's an unseemly tale to tell in the presence of a man like you," Oike was saying.

"Nonsense. Artists must be willing to bite into all the stories that fall from life's branches. Even the wormy ones," Kurobe laughed, and put his hand on the smaller man's shoulder to ease the sting of the remark. Then he continued thoughtfully: "Perhaps especially the wormy ones. Besides, I'm a puppeteer, Oike, not a court lady from Kyoto. You needn't worry about scandalizing me."

"Thank you for saying so, sir . . . Well, my father was a merchant in Osaka. I never wanted for anything when I was a boy. My parents, the servants and tutors, they all looked after me, everyone spoiled me I suppose, in spite of, you know, my condition, or maybe because of it, maybe they were trying to protect me from the world. But then something happened with my father. A business reversal. I never learned the circumstances, but we lost everything. And so naturally, my father, he did as any father would, he thought of family suicide, to spare us all the shame. I was thirteen. I remember him coming into my room. But he couldn't do it. At the last minute, he started . . . He became emotional. Asking forgiveness. For abandoning me, for leaving me to live with a disgraced name. He'd spoiled me too much, you see, he wasn't strong enough to do what he knew he should. He couldn't be strong with me. Just with my mother, and then himself . . . So after that I went to live with a cousin. Until he fell on his own hard times, and, well, to make a long story short, I ended up being sold to a traveling fair. We went all over. There was every sort of performer you could imagine. Even a puppeteer. A one-man show. Nothing like proper puppet theater, nothing like you, sir. No real art to it, just slapstick and the sort of humor I can't speak of here. But still I watched. And he talked to me sometimes, it turned out he knew about serious puppet drama as well, Chikamatsu's plays, for instance. And you, sir. He knew all about your work.

He taught me things. I loved the puppets, you see, I'd loved them ever since seeing your performance. I'd never forgotten you up on that stage with Matahei . . . So I listened and tried to learn what I could. But then . . . Sir?"

". . . Yes. Yes, go on."

"Well, but then the owner of the fair, he died, and the performers disbanded, and I was set free. Set free, but with nowhere to go really. I ended up on the street, I'm ashamed to say. A common beggar. Until I realized something while I was begging one day. At the fair, the others, they'd all performed, one way or another. They all *did* something, while I . . . You see, they kept me in a wagon, and they'd bring me out so folks could get a good look—most people of course had never seen anything like me— but I always just stood there uselessly and let them watch . . . It occurred to me, though, while I was begging that day, that maybe I could make use of my . . . of what I am. I could *do* something. *Perform* somehow. And I hit upon the idea. The basics of it. It's no surprise, I guess. Because puppetry was always with me. In my mind, I mean. I'd be there on the street, but a drama would be going on in my head, I'd be playing a show for myself. And so my act, that's when it began to . . ." Oike stopped. "I'm too ashamed to say any more, sir. That act of mine, it's not worth discussing. I'm sorry to have gone on for so long."

Kurobe said nothing. He was grateful for the darkness: for the last few moments he had been weeping silently as they walked. He had been moved to hear of how the father had spared his son; moved further when he learned of the various degradations Oike had endured, the story made all the more poignant by Oike's matter-of-fact telling of it, not a hint of self-pity in his voice. But the tears had come only when Oike began describing the act he had created. Kurobe remembered what he'd seen on the street, and this—being forced to make a mockery of what you love in order to survive—seemed the worst degradation of all.

Oike became a regular visitor. Kurobe and his new friend would talk late into the evening, and as time went on, Kurobe's daughter-in-law was ordered more and more frequently to prepare the guest room so Oike could stay the night. Kurobe was perhaps even guilty of half-deliberately keeping Oike late as an excuse to have him remain until morning. Certainly he was pleased with the result: for that night, at least, Oike had been spared sleeping on the street; but even more importantly, he had been prevented from performing his act.

Kurobe relished the chance to explain the nuances of his art to such an attentive pupil. His elder son's apprenticeship had been all distraction; his younger son's all duty. But now he had a listener whose silent attention seemed to reflect back to him his own passion for puppetry. He eventually realized, however, that he could go no further in his lessons without the use of an actual puppet. The construction of the Kurobe puppets and the techniques used to animate them were a family secret. Nevertheless, one day, in the midst of an explanation, Kurobe rose abruptly and left the room. When he returned he held the artist Matahei in his arms.

Oike seemed to hold his breath. Kurobe began to demonstrate some simple movements for his friend—parted lips; an extended hand; a pair of raised eyebrows—then turned the puppet around, exposing the opening in its back. "Go ahead, reach inside," Kurobe said, smiling. He expected Oike to be pleased; but the little man instantly recoiled. "No!" he cried sharply. "No, sir, I mustn't . . ." And shaking his head vigorously, he let out a strange laugh.

Kurobe was eventually able to coax Oike into stretching a tentative hand through the opening. He felt and finally held the stick; his fingers, though, were too short to reach the levers unassisted, so Kurobe placed his own hand over Oike's, and together they moved through first the basic controls and then the more advanced combinations; and Oike's face seemed to undergo its own subtle changes as the wooden face beside him changed from one expression to the next . . .

Ordinarily, Kurobe consulted with his younger son before making any important decisions concerning the theater. But one afternoon he called in Sojiro and curtly announced that Oike was to be taken on as an assistant. He thought afterward that he had perhaps been too short with his son, as if to swiftly stamp out an objection which had in fact never been raised. Sojiro merely bowed, said, "I understand, Father," and set about making preparations for Oike's arrival.

Oike was given a room in the Kurobe home and put to work as an assistant to the puppet-maker's apprentice. He was tolerated there without complaint, in keeping with Master Kurobe's wishes, although he was forbidden to handle the puppets themselves. Instead he was given simple tasks, and gradually allowed to observe the basic skills of puppet maintenance and repair. Kurobe knew there were murmurs, of course. At times he would make a surprise appearance in the workshop. "How is my little man doing, then?" he would say, laughing sheepishly. Or, "I hope my little man isn't causing trouble!"

When Oike's work was done Kurobe often invited him out to the pavilion. The two would sit there for hours while his daughter-in-law served tea and cake, talking about art or, at times, simply looking out together at the garden, imperfectly carpeted now with red and gold leaves.

As fall turned to winter, a change came over Kurobe. He did not exactly neglect his puppetry; he in any case knew his repertoire so thoroughly that he could have performed each part flawlessly without ever rehearsing again. But whereas in the past his free time had been spent with his puppets, now he found he preferred to spend that time with Oike, as if in a rush to impart to the little man all of his knowledge in the short time he had left.

One cold afternoon Kurobe was in the garden going over a scene from an upcoming performance with Mogi, the theater's narrator, when the name of the drama, and even the thread of the conversation, left him completely. He had the most annoying sense that the memory was circling just out of reach. If he had admitted his lapse, if he had apologized and laughed it off, the incident might have been forgotten. What aging man did not, after all, experience such moments? But he stiffened, and blinked, and remained perfectly silent as his humiliation deepened and the memory danced around him. Mogi said nothing, but Kurobe felt sure afterward that he knew, or suspected. He had no doubt that Mogi could be trusted with his secret—they had been friends for more than thirty years. He also realized, though, that it was only a matter of time now before the others—his fellow puppeteers, the puppet-makers, musicians, stage crew, and most critically, his sons—learned what was happening to him.

He needed to name a successor without further delay; but each time he reminded himself, he felt himself blanketed by a pleasant torpor which seemed to assure him that any danger was distant and small and hardly worthy of consideration.

Then spring came and, out walking with Oike beneath the cherry blossoms—petals fell like snowflakes, swirling at their feet, drifting across their path, and lodging, Kurobe could see, in Oike's sparse hair—his affliction once more took hold. It lifted him up and it set him back down again; and he was like a man who awakes and for a confusing instant cannot say where or when . . .

Pink: pink swirled around him. Pink branches above. Cherry blossoms: sign of spring. Spring, then . . . And beside him? Oike. It was Oike. He recognized him instantly, but with an absurd dream-sense of joy and nostalgia, as if he had just been reunited with a long-lost comrade.

Oike looked up and said only, "Sir?"

And then, as if he understood everything, he reached up, took Kurobe's hand, and led him through the pink snowfall.

After that Oike was constantly with the old master. The pair became a common sight on benches beside the river, on the streets surrounding the theater, even backstage before a performance. They spent many companionable hours together in the garden, although Kurobe now avoided the carp pool (he couldn't stand the sight of the Emperor's fish cutting its crazed lines through the water). Oike no longer assisted the puppet-maker. This pretense was ended; instead his days were devoted to remaining at the puppeteer's side.

One evening, after giving Oike an informal lecture on the forbidden puppet play *Love Suicides at Sonezaki*, banned now for more than a hundred years because of the real-life suicides it had inspired, Kurobe walked his friend to his door, said good night, and then, inexplicably, found himself confused as to where to go. He knew perfectly well that he was in his own home. Yet he had the most curious certainty that the rooms and doorways, the stairs and halls of his house—everything outside the range of his candle—had begun surreptitiously rearranging themselves.

He felt the way he had as a boy, watching his father rehearse while sets—castle walls; the gates of a shrine; a peasant cottage—glided on wooden tracks across the stage, and he would wait for them to slide into position, forming a scene he could recognize; now too it seemed as if the elements of his world had slid apart and were realigning; now too it seemed he was on the verge of recognizing something fundamental; he waited for it to be revealed to him, and when the sliding ceased and he found himself in a space both familiar and unknown—there was no way to know whether he should go left or right—the dwarflike creature before him studying his face, also familiar like a character from a half-remembered children's tale, gently took the candle from him—a guide, Kurobe understood, to the corridors of the reconfigured world . . .

❉   ❉   ❉

Kurobe soon recovered; but it nevertheless became a nightly custom for Oike, candle in hand, to walk the old man to his door. One night, as he was returning afterward to his own room, someone fell into step behind him. Oike turned to find Kurobe's elder son in the darkness just beyond the candlelight, grinning down at him.

"'Evening," Genzo said.

"Good evening, sir."

"It stopped raining, finally. Feels like it's cooled off some out there. I thought I might take a walk. Care to join me?"

Together they trudged through the mud. Genzo strode purposefully ahead, stepping over puddles while Oike followed, skirting them as best he could. They passed darkened houses, crossed a bridge, and came to an area of wet cobbled streets.

Pink lanterns bobbed gaily in the breeze, marking the borders of the pleasure quarter.

"What do you say to a drink?" Genzo asked.

Oike wasn't used to drinking, at least not in the quantities Kurobe's son consumed. Genzo nevertheless cheerfully demanded that Oike match him cup for cup. An hour hadn't gone by before the little man needed to be hauled over Genzo's shoulder like a sack of rice. Twice Oike was sick on the way home, once right down the back of Genzo's kimono. Genzo, though, only laughed. The following night, Genzo again waited until his father had retired, fell quietly into step behind Oike, and invited him out for a walk. Oike tried to decline, claiming to have been under the weather all day; but Genzo insisted. So off they went; and this time it took three more cups of sake before Genzo's new drinking companion needed to be slung over a shoulder and carried home.

It wasn't long before Oike—who had given up on trying to refuse and now accompanied Kurobe's son with a look of resignation—became capable of putting away as much as a man twice his size, and the night came when Oike left the tavern on his own small pair of feet. Genzo found this turn of events, which he hadn't anticipated, very amusing. He kept bending over and, patting (or rather clumsily slapping) Oike on the head and shoulders, loudly congratulating him. He suggested they celebrate Oike's achievement; and, weaving perhaps even more than Oike himself, led the little man to a nearby geisha house.

At first Oike seemed uncomfortable there, but after a few more drinks he was even cajoled into performing an unsteady impromptu rendition of his street act. This went over tremendously well with not only the geishas but the other customers as well. Everyone laughed and cheered. Oike had known only the streets of the pleasure quarter; but as the weeks passed, Genzo began inviting him into all of the bright festive worlds that had until then remained hidden behind high walls and closed doors. Genzo was a well-known and—when he hadn't over-extended himself—well-paying customer; with him as escort, Oike was guaranteed admission to establishments which would otherwise certainly have turned him away. Genzo, for his part, found that his new friend's presence won him entry once again into places from which he had himself been barred for one sake-inspired misbehavior or other. He brought with him, after all, an irresistible novelty; and once Oike was drunk enough (and these days he never failed to become fabulously, gloriously drunk) he would, without any prompting, leap up on the nearest table to dance, show magic tricks, or perform bawdy parodies of puppet theater.

Occasionally, Genzo allowed himself to wonder why he was spending so much time with Oike.

When he first discovered him on the street, Genzo had recognized something in the little man's act. It appeared there for an instant amid all the grotesquerie: an anomaly of some sort—a movement? an expression? he couldn't say—that had brought to mind his father's puppetry. Art peeking out, as if by accident, from the moronic clowning; and by the time he began watching Oike in earnest, by the time he tried to examine what he was seeing, it was already gone. He'd felt a desire—an obligation almost—to share with his father what he'd witnessed. But there was no way to explain it really, even to himself; so he'd offered to take his father to see the act. True, maybe he was a little drunk at the time, but did that make his offer any less genuine? Drink or no drink, it had taken courage, after everything that had passed between them. A hand reached out to his father. Reached out, and slapped away: *You know perfectly well that's not the sort of place where I choose to spend my time.* And then to be compared to a dog . . . After finishing his bottle of sake he'd stumbled out onto the street, bent on finding the deformed creature: if his father wouldn't go with him to see his discovery, he'd bring the damned thing home. A prank; a small revenge. And the next day had gone marvelously: his father's initial outrage at the sight of Oike had been a moment to savor; but best of all had been Genzo's vindication, which occurred the moment the little man, quite on his own and without any encouragement, stood up and enacted the scene from *Shogen's House*: there it was, plainly written on his father's stunned (and even strangely stricken) face: proof that he had recognized the same talent Genzo had spoken of all along.

The matter should have ended there. But then Oike was invited back. And not only once but again and again. Genzo hadn't foreseen this. Oike was an entertaining enough character, and his knowledge of puppet theater really *was* extraordinary; but for him to be taken on as assistant and installed in their home . . . ! Before long the creature never left his father's side. And the way his father doted on him . . . The prank had taken on a life of its own. And it was all Genzo's own doing. He arrived at a sort of plan to make things right, although its contours remained unclear to him even as he carried it out. He was trying, he understood eventually, to drown his father's new confidant in sake, to keep him drunk at night and hungover by day, until his father became so disgusted he would send the filthy little thing packing, back to the streets where he belonged. Genzo had wanted to destroy the unsettling friendship between the two, but equally he'd wanted his father to know that Genzo was the instrument of that destruction.

Yet somewhere along the way the plan had revised itself. He'd come to look forward to his time with Oike; he was no longer sure what he wanted. Did his father know about their nights together? If he did he gave no sign. Had Oike kept it a secret? Or had he already confessed everything: the sake, the geisha houses, the drunken tabletop parodies of puppet theater? If it *was* a secret, it wouldn't be a difficult one to keep from his father these days. He sometimes hardly seemed aware of what was happening around him. He could be in the room with you and not see you there at all. It was true he'd always had a distracted quality, like any man absorbed in his work. But behind it there had been a focus, a sense that his mind was elsewhere, perhaps, but fully engaged; now there was a vagueness to his distraction that worried Genzo.

And then one evening during a performance of *Chushingura*, in the middle of Kanpei's suicide scene, something happened to his father. Not an error, exactly. A hesitation; a missed beat. An instant when father and sons were no longer moving together in unison.

A voice within Genzo had always foretold dissolution. Even as a boy, he could sense the ruin waiting in every bright shape that bloomed around him. When his mother died, Genzo's father accused him of failing to properly mourn, seeing his wild revels as evidence that he wasn't grieving, or worse—that he was celebrating his own mother's death. One more thing that could not be forgiven. It wasn't true, of course; but he had experienced . . . Not joy, certainly, but—well, a balm of sorts, a consolation: yes, everything really was meant to end in collapse, as he'd always suspected. After the cremation, they took turns, the three of them—his father, then Genzo, then Sojiro—removing her bones. Striving: this is what it came to, when all was said and done. Bones picked from ashes with a pair of chopsticks. As if her death were an argument won, his view of the world confirmed and his father's disproven once and for all. And so he waited for a similar consolation now at seeing the great Master Kurobe finally falter, a consolation he felt sure he should be feeling . . .

He wondered if Sojiro had also detected his father's hesitation; but he kept what he'd noticed to himself. Was there some connection between his father's strangeness and the rumors of retirement? Genzo had always had mixed feelings about succession. The expectations, the ludicrous and arcane formalities, the endless stultifying daily chores of managing a theater—in short, all that went with being his father's successor—he'd wanted no part of it. And so the talk of retiring, even if only heard secondhand, had made him anxious. Yet it was also true that he'd secretly dreamed of becoming lead puppeteer for years. He hated being restricted onstage to the manipulation of the puppet's left hand; it gave him a feeling of paralysis, as though everything of importance to him could only be expressed through a single limb. Sometimes after a particularly long show, which could last nearly a day, the feeling persisted for hours, the sense that he had control of only his left hand, which throbbed with agonizing life, while the rest of him remained wooden and inert . . . Like an injured man impatient to recover, to rise and unwind the bandages, he'd waited—without ever quite admitting it to himself—for the time when he could gain the use of the puppet's entire body. When he could lead rather than follow. But now that the moment seemed to be approaching, his entire being was seized with alarm. He hoped the feeling would pass, but with each day its hold on him felt more secure, as if it were slowly passing through layers of flesh to grip his bones.

He asked Oike oblique questions, trying to draw out information about his father's recent behavior; but no matter how much Genzo plied him with sake, Oike said nothing. (The sake, in any case, no longer seemed to have much of an effect.)

After Oike had finished performing his act in a tavern one night, a customer, recognizing Genzo, pointed at him and shouted:

"Look! It's a Kurobe! We've been watching the puppet, but here's the master. And even better than his father. He can control a puppet without even touching it!"

Laughing, the man slapped his thigh, applauding not Oike but Genzo. Others joined in the mock applause. Feeling flushed and a bit giddy, Genzo jumped to his feet and, with a grin, thrust a hand between Oike's shoulder blades as if clutching hidden controls there. This brought a roar of laughter. But Oike's reaction—a stillness as he studied the watching faces, then a stiffening and a slow bend at the waist, until it was no longer Oike but a puppet bowing before them—brought an even greater roar.

Out of this improvised scene, which had started as nothing but a drunken joke, grew their two-man routine. Oike, as before, stood on a tabletop, acting the part of the puppet. But now Genzo kneeled behind him, one hand on Oike's spine and the other at his elbow, playing the role of puppeteer. They performed it casually at first, when requested, at taverns or geisha houses. As word spread, however, they were surprised to receive invitations first to the better homes of the city, and finally even to the lacquered halls of the local nobility, although always after dark and always with a clandestine air surrounding the event, generated in large part by the hosts themselves, who experienced thereby a titillating sense of transgression. The two men came to enjoy a certain celebrity, if a rather unseemly one. The humor of the situation, of course, was not lost on Genzo, nor on his audiences: Oike accompanied Master Kurobe through one world by day, then accompanied his son through another world by night. By now everyone knew about the old puppeteer's deformed companion, and they assumed the act was a prank, a wicked parody by the son at the legendary father's expense; the winking cruelty of it, the flavor of scandal, was no doubt a central part of the performance's appeal. And it was true that, during the routine, Genzo would find himself impersonating his father, down to his most distinctive mannerisms; whether this was in fact a parody of his father, however, or something else altogether he couldn't have said himself.

Over time the act became formalized, although the two men never once discussed it together, as if too ashamed to speak of the matter aloud. Oike began to eliminate the jerky puppet-movements of his past performances, replacing them with gestures of nearly human smoothness; he retained only the slightest rigidity to lend a trace of verisimilitude to his characterization. The two moved together so well Genzo was almost able to imagine that he was genuinely controlling Oike, that Oike's poses and expressions were flowing from Genzo's own hands into the tiny figure before him; and he thought at times he could see in Oike's movements the life he knew he could bring to his art if awarded the title of Master Puppeteer.

Late one evening, after performing their act at an exclusive geisha house, Genzo took Oike to his first brothel. When he suggested the visit, Oike acquiesced as always, but with a curious expression on his shrunken face. As they approached, Oike slowed, hesitating. He stopped on the front step.

"What is it?" Genzo asked.

"I'm repulsive."

"Well, yes, of course you are," Genzo laughed, "but they're *whores*, Oike. Don't you see? No matter how monstrous you look—no matter how monstrous you *are*, inside or out—they'll still accept you. With open arms! That's the whole point."

And he gave his friend a kindly shove through the doorway.

The surprising thing was that the whores didn't seem to find Oike repulsive at all. On the contrary, after recovering from their surprise they surrounded him, ignoring Genzo altogether as they dropped to their knees to coo and poke and pat his tiny companion like children who've been presented with a rare and beautiful doll. And Oike's face and body had in fact gone as rigid as if carved of wood. Finally he was lifted by a circle of hands, undressed, bathed, and paraded around the front room swaddled in towels, Oike looking terrified and his captors laughing deliriously all the while.

Genzo had been prepared to pay for Oike, but the little man was carried off to a room free of charge. The same thing occurred each time they visited: Genzo paid for himself like any ordinary customer, while Oike ended up in the arms of one giggling whore or other without so much as a coin changing hands. For a while, each took her turn; then the brothel's greatest beauty, who went by the name of Princess Tachibana, began to take an interest in Oike. When he arrived, she would squeal with delight, snatch him up, and bundle him off to her no doubt lavishly appointed chamber before the others could lay a hand on him. Genzo had always been a little bit in love with Princess Tachibana—this was why he never chose her—and he couldn't help but feel a pang of envy watching Oike being swept up like a child into an adoring mother's arms. More than once, as he left the brothel alone, he found himself wondering, and even imagining, what was going on between the two at that moment in the Princess's chamber.

On one of these nights, wandering forlorn and dejected from the brothel out onto the streets, he discovered that his feet had led him to a familiar door. He had already run up a substantial debt there, but the manager welcomed him back with a bow and promptly granted more credit. A dozen rolls of the dice later, Genzo rose and made his way back out into the night. Moonlight coated every surface like a layer of frost. He walked through deserted streets. The bridge, the rows of darkened houses: they moved serenely past, as if nothing had happened. He looked at his own dark house. Finally he went inside, but without the usual panache—the drunken stamping of feet, the fanfare of slamming doors, all the ways he had of announcing his late arrival. He entered quietly and slipped through the house, wary as a burglar.

In the days and weeks that followed he stayed away from the quarter, in part out of a desire for expiation, and in part due to a more practical consideration: he feared being spotted. It was no longer prudent to be seen spending money now that his debt had tripled. When he did finally return—it wasn't realistic, after all, to keep punishing himself forever—it was to quiet places on the fringe of the quarter. He went alone. Princess Tachibana now claimed Oike's nights. Genzo began to suspect that she had found a way to make use of Oike in her work. There were rumors of special performances for select customers; he heard talk of an exotic act which could be viewed or even joined in for a certain price. It eventually became clear that these were not merely rumors: in the quarter's lantern-lit world, the act known as "Princess Tachibana Playing with Her Favorite Doll" began to acquire a notoriety that eclipsed the brief fame Genzo and Oike had enjoyed as puppeteer and puppet. In one of his visits to the quarter's edge he learned something else which turned out to be more than a rumor: Shinoda himself—the man who controlled most of the quarter's brothels and gambling dens, and the man to whom Genzo ultimately owed his debt—was looking for him. After this he had no choice but to avoid the pleasure quarter completely, even though he had more time on his hands than ever now that the theater had gone on hiatus (something to do apparently with one of the shamisen players).

Then one day his brother asked to speak with him. He thought at first that Sojiro had learned about the debt, and prepared himself for a chiding: it wouldn't be so easy this time, he knew, for his brother to simply step in and help the way he usually did. Sojiro's face was as unreadable as ever; but even before they'd taken their places on the mat, Genzo began to sense that this concerned a different matter entirely.

❀　❀　❀

Sojiro had been observing their father closely for quite some time. And he had witnessed certain . . . *peculiarities* he felt the brothers could no longer afford to ignore. Certain lapses. He made the case point by point, citing numerous small instances which taken together proved, or at least strongly supported, his case. He omitted only one example, although it was the most significant of all: several months before, during a performance of *Chushingura: The Treasury of Loyal Retainers*, just when Sojiro was about to take the puppet's feet a diagonal half step forward, he had felt in his father a delay, a hesitation which lasted for nearly a full beat. Sojiro had mentioned nothing to his brother at the time. And now, without knowing why, he found himself leaving it out of his argument.

"So there it is." Sojiro rested his hands on his thighs and looked down at the mat. He waited for Genzo to speak. To take the lead. To behave, for once, like an older brother. But when he glanced up, Genzo was pale and stricken, as if suddenly suffering an especially bad hangover; leaning forward, he whispered, "Have you spoken to Father about this?"

And on his face a guilty look. The look of a collaborator.

"I'm afraid we're past that point," Sojiro replied, his voice louder than intended, as if to show anyone who might be eavesdropping—though he'd made sure the house was empty—that he was not ashamed, that he was not colluding in some sort of plot.

Sojiro did not tell his brother, but he had in fact gone to their father a week before. He would never have approached Genzo about such an important matter without having spoken to their father first.

He'd found him in the tea room with Oike.

"I'm sorry to intrude. Could I have a word with you, Father? Privately?"

His father seemed prepared to be outraged; but Oike instantly rose and, bowing, left the room before his father could complain.

"There's a matter we need to discuss. Concerning the theater."

"The theater?" His father looked at him.

"Yes. It's . . ." He had rehearsed his speech. He had considered carefully the proper wording, the most sensitive and respectful way to broach the subject. Instead, he said:

"It's Fujita, the shamisen player. It seems there's been some sort of family crisis. He has to return to Nara. I'm afraid we'll need to go on hiatus."

Many years later, when Sojiro was himself an old man and had forgotten much of the unpleasant business that followed (and numerous other incidents in his life as well), he still remembered this moment. He had never lied to his father before. He'd known speaking up would be difficult, but had believed, until now, that his sense of duty would prove stronger than the momentary shame of confronting his father.

"A crisis?" his father said. "What kind of crisis?"

"He wouldn't say. He may not return."

"Surely we can replace him."

"Not on such short notice. I've made inquiries, but . . . Just a brief hiatus. A temporary closing, until we can find a suitable replacement. A rest, for everyone . . ."

He felt his father studying him.

"And you think this is the only way?"

"Yes, Father."

His father was silent. When he finally gave his consent, it was not with a word but with a brief nod that seemed directed as much at himself as at his son.

"The other performers," he said, "they'll have to be told immediately, of course. And the public: it's a delicate matter, the phrasing of the announcement. Even a temporary closing like this—it's not to be taken lightly. There are many things to be considered." He paused. "As you know." He nodded again. "I leave it all to you."

Of course, Fujita now had to be released. He was a skilled player, and Sojiro was sorry to see him go. After being told of "unforeseen circumstances" requiring a brief hiatus, he was paid well—as much as he would have earned in a full season of performances—and sent home to Nara. Sojiro hurried him off, personally escorting him as far as the outskirts of the city to ensure that he spoke with no one. Then it was simply a matter of repeating to the theater's staff the story he had told his father. In this way Sojiro was able to bring about the closing of the theater without anyone suspecting the real reason.

The incident nevertheless left him shaken: the lying; the dejected look on Fujita's face; the finality of his father's nod. He was able to convince himself in the end that he had after all done only what was necessary. If the entire situation continued to trouble him, it was for another reason: he had, until now, never acted on his own. Though for years he had managed the day-to-day business of the theater, his father had always been consulted before any truly significant decision. Sojiro was unable to imagine a future without his father there to let him know what was required of him . . .

Naturally he'd heard the rumors of retirement. But he didn't trust rumors. Rumors were like superstition: they had a way of coming true once you let yourself believe in them. Sojiro had never had time for such nonsense. He preferred reason to folk wisdom, established facts to murmured half-truths. If his father were seriously considering retirement, he would tell Sojiro when the time was right. It was just a matter of waiting. Still, it was natural to think, occasionally, about the rumors, if only so he could apply reason to dismiss them once and for all. Take, for instance, his father's rumored inability to choose between the brothers. This hardly seemed plausible. It wouldn't be true to say that he had ever coveted the title of lead puppeteer, but at the same time he had never questioned that it was his destiny. What he did or did not want in any case hardly seemed relevant. His brother might have been the elder son, but he had disqualified himself long ago, no matter how much Sojiro tried to hide his faults—looking after him the way you would an idiot or a child, steering him to his room when he was drunk, nursing him through his hangovers, propping him up so that he seemed to stand respectably on his own, as when Sojiro quietly paid off his brother's debts before they threatened once more to endanger the family name. Sojiro had, practically since childhood, been convinced of the inevitability of his accession, if only by default. Much of his life had therefore consisted of preparation for a duty he had taken for granted would need to be taken on, even if his father had never said so explicitly.

But what if the rumors *were* true? If his father did plan to retire, why hadn't he already awarded the title to Sojiro? There were, as far as he could determine, three possibilities, and he examined each in turn: (1) his father's indecision was more evidence of failing faculties (although he still seemed, for the most part, very much himself, and it was difficult to believe him utterly incapable of making an important choice such as this); (2) his father was reluctant to violate the tradition of passing title to the eldest son; or (3) his father had some secret preference for Genzo himself. It was with this third possibility that Sojiro's powers of analysis shook into collapse around him . . . How could he begin to account for such a possibility? Had he in some way inadvertently neglected his duty? Had he failed his father? Or was it more . . . fundamental? He'd once overheard his father talking with Mogi the narrator; his father had said— No: there was no point in remembering; no point in speculating. This was all supposition. He had no intention of letting useless thoughts take possession of him. He was, in any case, prepared to obey regardless of who was chosen, prepared to obey even if he didn't understand, provided he could receive some indication of his father's desire.

He had hoped that the temporary closing of the theater

would prompt a decision. But there were no changes, no announcements. His father seemed in no particular hurry to return to the stage, either, which was in itself unusual. (In the past, even a high fever wouldn't keep him from performing. Once his father had gone onstage—over the objections of Sojiro's mother—in spite of a terrible infection in one leg.) His days, as always, were spent with Oike. Sojiro waited. He continued to wait even though he knew the theater had been closed now for too long. Weeks had passed; soon the rumors would begin; shamisen players were not, after all, so hard to replace. And there were rival theaters to consider . . . Still Sojiro waited. He waited at first for his father to announce his retirement and name his successor. And then, losing faith in his father, he waited for a sign to let him know what he should do . . .

After the theater had been closed for nearly two months, an incident finally occurred which seemed like the sign he'd been waiting for. It involved a cucumber seed. His father was in the habit of eating with his dinner thinly sliced cucumbers marinated in soy sauce. On this particular evening his father ate them, as usual. Midway through the meal, though, he became irate: glaring around the table, he demanded to know why his cucumbers hadn't been served to him. Sojiro's wife apologized, pretending to have forgotten, and rushed toward the kitchen. At this moment his father looked down at his sauce dish and saw there, floating in the brown liquid, a single green seed. For a moment he stared down at the seed. Then he roared, and would certainly have overturned the table if his sons hadn't restrained him. Sojiro tried his best to make his father see reason. But in the end it was Oike who proved able to calm him, whispering into his ear a few words Sojiro couldn't make out . . .

After dinner Sojiro bowed and thanked Oike for his assistance. But the more he thought about Oike's role in "the cucumber seed incident" (as he'd come to think of it), the more disturbing it became. Certainly Oike had helped. Yet wasn't there something odd in his ability to so easily pacify his father? A few whispered words . . . It seemed to hint at some inexplicable power of control . . . He had, of course, had reservations about Oike from the beginning, particularly once he was given a place in their home; but it had seemed a harmless enough if uncharacteristic indulgence on his father's part, as if he had decided to take in a three-legged stray found hobbling outside the garden. And Oike was nothing if not innocuous. He never spoke out of turn. He rarely spoke at all; meek and inoffensive, one could almost forget he was there. At least until his father began coddling the creature like a belated third son. Sojiro had hardly known what to make of it . . . Only now, though, did he begin to see something sinister in Oike's presence there. Upon consideration, wasn't it true that his father's decline had coincided with Oike's arrival? It would be easy to go too far with this: he considered and rejected as improbable, for instance, the notion that Oike might have been polluting his father's mind with a potion slipped into his food or drink. Still, might there not be some species of psychological poisoning, some malevolent influence? . . . Words whispered like a spell . . . At the very least, Oike's arrival had signaled bad luck, as if he were an omen. Or a curse.

The cucumber seed incident, if nothing else, established irrefutably the need for action regarding his father. Like a tongue tapping compulsively at a sore on the roof of the mouth, Sojiro's mind kept returning against its will to that painful moment; and he found that each successive tap brought greater certainty concerning what was required of him: he felt himself moving into closer alignment with a force—or rather a *presence* (familiar to him, although he couldn't yet identify it)—ready to direct and counsel him . . . If he had believed himself to be acting on his own, it all would have been overwhelming; but he began to sense that he was only an instrument of that unnamed presence, and this realization helped immeasurably as he began making what would otherwise have been difficult decisions in the days that followed . . .

The first step was to inform the public that Master Kurobe had taken ill. The nature of the illness, of course, was left unmentioned. Sojiro reported the news without gravity, describing it as a minor complaint which, however, required him to remain in bed. As a result, his father had to be kept at home, and his walks restricted to the garden; but this turned out not to be a problem—his father showed little interest now in going out in any case. Sojiro hadn't anticipated, though, the number of neighbors, theater performers, and assorted important figures who would come to pay their respects. They had to be told that his father was refusing to take visitors. Old Mogi the narrator was especially insistent, nearly demanding to be let in. These scenes left Sojiro humiliated; but his victory in subduing the guests with courtesy gave him courage. It was the presence he had discovered within him: it was lending him the strength to face such indignities.

The next step was the naming of a successor; Sojiro, of course, would need to make this decision on his father's behalf. He knew that he was the more capable of the brothers; still, he was reluctant to put himself forward in his brother's place, however much Genzo might have wished for such a thing. It seemed dishonorable. Besides, the public would expect the title to pass to Genzo, and not only because he was the eldest. Sojiro was well aware that his brother was considered the more talented of the sons. Years before, he had overheard his father talking one day to Mogi. The narrator had just finished praising Genzo's natural ability, and his father had said: "Well yes, he might have the talent, that one; but that's about all he has. And I don't need to tell you, it takes more than just raw talent to amount to anything as an artist."

No matter how qualified the compliment, his father's words had surprised him. Where was this talent everyone spoke of? In knowledge, in mastery of technique, he was clearly his brother's superior. And what was puppetry if not the gradual and orderly accumulation of expertise? It was an art, some might say. But it had always seemed to Sojiro that art was simply a word people used when they were unable to properly define something. When they spoke of his brother's talent, people were really trying to give a name to some capricious quality they imagined might mysteriously surface in his brother when he wasn't drunk or distracted. Perhaps his father—perhaps everyone—saw Sojiro's own talents as uninspired by comparison; but can a career be built, let alone sustained, on caprice and mystery?

Such thoughts had continued to trouble him long after hearing his father's words. Now, though, it all seemed like childish nonsense. He was no longer interested in aesthetic arguments or sibling rivalry; his only concern was his obligation to the family name and business. The most important consideration was continuing to fill the theater now that his father was gone; and whatever one might say about his brother and his abilities—call it raw talent or art or simply charisma—he certainly knew how to attract attention. His reputation, even his infamy, might very well draw crowds. Nevertheless, allowing Genzo control of the theater, and particularly its finances, would be catastrophic. With his habits it would only be a matter of months before the business was driven into the ground and the Kurobe name disgraced. At first it seemed as though there was no solution; then an answer appeared, and it was so obvious that it seemed as though it had been present, waiting to be discovered, all along.

His father's stamp, an announcement to the public, a brief ceremony, and it was over: this was all it took for title to pass from father to son. Succession, in the end, amounted to nothing more than that. The difficult part had been persuading his brother. Impossible, Genzo kept repeating, eyes as frantic as those of a child who knows he must take his medicine but still feverishly hopes for escape. "You know me. Master Puppeteer? . . . No. No: impossible. Don't you realize? I'll ruin everything." He said this hopelessly, shaking his head with self-hatred; but Sojiro understood that it was also a threat.

He immediately set about reassuring his brother: Sojiro would manage all of the mundane tasks necessary to keep the theater operating: the finances, the advertising, the practical details and the formal niceties, the supervision of performers and crew—Genzo needn't concern himself with any of that. Freed from these responsibilities, Genzo could concentrate instead on the theater's artistic direction. In other words, he could expect to receive all of the honors associated with the rank of Master Puppeteer, honors to which he was after all entitled as elder son; the actual duties, however, would be shared equally between the brothers.

Genzo's mouth squirmed.

"All right," he said finally, his body sagging, though it was unclear whether from relief or surrender. "And I can count on you, little brother?"

"Of course. Always."

If Sojiro had been tempted, however briefly, to inform his father and seek his blessing, the man, he reminded himself, showed no interest now in his legacy or in the fate of his theater; he was content to sit vacantly for hours, Oike like an ever-present parasite fattening beside him, slowly draining him of his wits. Sojiro had come to realize that this man was no longer in any real sense his father at all; he had become an impostor, a trespasser in their home no less than Oike himself. Though there were still times when he behaved exactly as their father had, times when he seemed perfectly reasonable, this was no more than a kind of deception. Sojiro had finally identified the nameless presence that had been guiding him ever since the cucumber seed incident: it was his father, it had been his father all along—his *real* father—or rather the essence of him, his wishes and his wisdom, directing Sojiro's actions as surely as if his father's spirit had risen out of the empty-eyed remnant there on the mat and come to inhabit Sojiro instead.

Preparations were made for the theater's reopening. Now that Genzo had been promoted to control of the puppet's head and right hand, another puppeteer took over the task of operating the left hand; Sojiro remained in charge of the feet. Genzo had suggested that Sojiro himself move up to the more prestigious left-hand position, but he preferred to stay where he'd always been, leading the steps of the Kurobe puppets in the proper direction.

For the moment at least, Genzo appeared willing enough to take on his new duties; during rehearsals, he even seemed excited by the role of lead puppeteer. Sojiro's concern, as always, was his brother's carousing. In due course a suitable wife would need to be chosen for him; it would be unseemly for a Master Puppeteer to remain unmarried. Besides, there was the important statement that a marriage would make: the formerly wayward son had settled into his new responsibility, marrying and—Sojiro hoped—eventually providing a son to carry on the family tradition. As to his brother's excessive spending, Sojiro had already taken the step of placing him on a limited allowance, explaining the need for frugality until the theater reestablished itself in the eyes of the public. But such measures could provide only a partial solution. And there was still the issue of Genzo's outstanding debt: word had reached Sojiro that his brother owed an enormous amount as a result of his gambling.

Sojiro had never met Shinoda. In the past, he had paid off his brother's debts through intermediaries; but he knew the man by reputation, and was prepared for the worst when he finally arranged to see him. Shinoda was younger than Sojiro had expected, and far more gracious. He had a particular manner about him—affable yet without any trace of presumption. While an assistant poured tea, he said: "Thank you for coming. I know your theater must keep you very busy. Let me express, right from the outset, my willingness to resolve this. After all, the present situation benefits no one. As I'm sure you'd agree."

"Yes."

"I'd actually hoped to talk with your brother, but . . ." He paused tactfully, then went on: "We haven't been graced by his presence in the quarter these days. But now that you've kindly come in his place, to hear my proposal . . ."

"I am not here in my brother's place. In fact he doesn't know I've come. I'm here out of duty to my family's interests."

"Of course. I completely understand," Shinoda said, eyeing him with a peculiar grin. "So: to business?"

Sojiro had come ready to pay off Genzo's debt, or at least to negotiate a reasonable payment schedule. It soon became clear, though, that the "business" Shinoda referred to concerned more than just his brother's gambling—it concerned Oike, of all people. It seemed that Oike had gained a reputation in the quarter, was even in great demand for a certain exotic act he took part in, and Shinoda believed he could make profitable use of Oike's unique qualities and talents in an entertainment venture he was at that moment developing. Shinoda, in short, saw Oike as a valuable commodity, and was prepared to offer complete forgiveness of Genzo's debt in return for possession of Oike along with all performance rights.

Sojiro was about to correct Shinoda, who had somehow arrived at the ridiculous conclusion that Oike *belonged* to the Kurobe family; but was it really so far-fetched to claim that his family had—if in an admittedly rather indirect way— essentially arrived at something akin to ownership of the creature? They provided him, after all, with food and lodging, and allowed him every benefit normally reserved only for the immediate family itself. And all without any compensation. If not for them, Oike would still be a street tramp. Surely there had been an understanding between the creature and his father, a sort of unwritten contract: proper care in exchange for loyal companionship and all the privileges of possession. How else to explain the strange bond between the two?

Nevertheless, the idea of what they appeared to be discussing was so nonsensical that Sojiro had to resist a rare impulse to laugh out loud. It was all too absurd to be taken seriously. But the laugh he suppressed was not unmixed with terror: Shinoda didn't want money; Shinoda wanted Oike. Still, wouldn't Sojiro—if he'd thought of it—in fact have been willing to offer

Oike at no cost, or even to pay to have his family rid of the creature? All debt forgiven. Yes; but beyond that: a curse lifted, the
house swept clean, the little demon exorcised once and for all.
Of course it was mad; but in the playacting that this meeting
had become (for that was what it was; what else could it be?)
he felt emboldened to take on the part of Shrewd Haggler. The
premise: Oike as a valuable commodity. A thought occurred to
him: even if the debt were forgiven, it was only a matter of time
before his brother would return to the quarter to dig himself an
even deeper hole. But if . . . He began to speak tentatively, as if
thinking aloud: assuming for the moment that an arrangement
regarding Oike were possible: if he could suggest something
in the way of a provision, so to speak: if his brother were to be
banned from Shinoda-san's various places of business—that is
to say, banned in perpetuity—it would prevent any potential
recurrence of the present unpleasantness . . . Only now did he
glance across the table, feeling suddenly that the playacting had
gone too far; but Shinoda assented instantly with a dismissive
flick of the hand, seeming both contemptuous and embarrassed, as if Sojiro had committed some fundamental breach of
business etiquette by bringing up a mere detail in the midst of
serious negotiations.

The nature of the proposed agreement appeared now all at
once before Sojiro like a document prepared far in advance;
there was no paper—Shinoda insisted there was no need for
it between honorable men—but what was being presented to
him felt nevertheless as tangible, as unquestionably real, as a
page placed in his hand for final approval: his brother's debt,
including accrued interest, would be canceled forthwith, and
in addition Genzo would be permanently barred from any
and all of Shinoda's businesses; in exchange, legal ownership

of Oike would pass to Shinoda within a twenty-four-hour period.

Agreed?

Sojiro felt himself nod. And then, in a sort of panic, as if he had just pressed down the family stamp and then thought of an amendment, he began hurriedly begging for assurances that Shinoda's man would be discreet and kindly wait in the garden—excuse the rudeness—since Sojiro hoped to invite, or not invite, of course, but order, quietly order Oike out into the garden, but quietly, that was the point, everyone must act quietly, so as not to alert or, rather, alarm his family needlessly . . .

"Discretion: that goes without saying," Shinoda said. He produced a bottle of sake and two cups. "Speaking of which. Allow me to throw in a final gift, just to seal our arrangement: your brother, I can promise you, will never know about your part in any of this."

He made the offer casually as he set the cups on the table. Sojiro had intended to refuse the sake—he never drank—but upon hearing Shinoda's words, he was so overcome with relief and gratitude that he found himself allowing his cup to be filled.

"To brothers and brotherhood!" Shinoda cried.

Afterward, Sojiro stepped out into the afternoon, dazzled by the sunlight and strangely elated. He couldn't quite define to himself how he felt since it was entirely unfamiliar, but if he could have given it a name he might have said that he felt free. It had been his intention to return home as soon as his business was concluded, but instead he allowed himself to wander the quarter for the first time. The shops were still shuttered, the streets empty except for the occasional deliveryman pulling carts of food and sake for the coming night's revelry; but, peering through a gate's slats at a teahouse recessed in shadow, plunging on impulse into a mossy maze of alleys, the soft gurgle of water always elusively near, gazing up at the wooden sign-blocks dangling above a doorway, each bearing the fanciful stage name of a geisha—*Silken Wing; Moon Blossom; Silent Song*—he was able to imagine the splendors of the quarter at night, when this would all be transformed, everything hidden here revealed under the pink lanterns twirling overhead . . .

He wandered for a long time, until it was nearly evening. Then he abruptly stopped; remembered himself; and, reddening, turned and hurried home, already scolding himself for having wasted half the day.

❀　　❀　　❀

After Oike's disappearance, Kurobe rarely left his room. His time was spent alone, staring out the window at his garden. He didn't react when his daughter-in-law set a tray down before him; he didn't respond when asked hesitantly if he needed anything. He had ignored Chiyo often enough in the past as well, but now he seemed to find her presence there an unforgivable intrusion.

She did her best to act as if nothing had changed: she used the same honorific language as always; she bowed when she entered; bowed again when she left. After a month of this, she was almost glad to hear once more the familiar sound of orders barked from his room—"Tangerines!" or "Tea!" or "Where is my dinner?"

He finally began to leave his room on occasion, if only to wander the house as though searching for something. Her husband, encountering him by chance in a hallway or on the stairs, found his behavior especially disturbing. Sometimes she would find her father-in-law's window flung wide open, the room empty; he would be in the garden, gazing furiously into the pond. There was a concern that he might try to go out through the garden gates and end up lost in the streets. The gate could be sealed; but what was to keep him from climbing over the wall? . . . And then, one afternoon, he was discovered thrashing in the carp pool, soaking wet, apparently intent on snatching one of the fish from the water. When questioned about it, he refused to answer. He was—or so it seemed to Chiyo—becoming crafty in his silence, so that it was hard to know how much of him remained.

Her husband made a decision: it was no longer safe to allow his aimless roaming through the house and garden. He was moved to a storage room with a window too small for him to escape through. One of the doors was nailed shut; a stick in the rail of the other prevented it being slid open from within. Occasionally the door would rattle; once there was a pounding and a muffled shout; but for the most part he seemed content enough inside. Everything had been made as comfortable as possible, his furniture and belongings arranged just as they had been in his former room. Chiyo noticed, though, that there were no puppets. During dinner one evening, she suggested that her father-in-law might like to have one.

After a silence the brothers—first her husband and then her brother-in-law—resumed eating.

"I can't see the point in it," her husband said eventually. "He has no use for any of that now." (She had noticed how her husband chose the word "he" these days instead of "Father.") "Besides, we have no puppets to spare."

They finished dinner without another word. Chiyo was getting up to clear the table when her husband, looking at no one in particular, said, "There's probably a practice puppet some-where we could do without."

Chiyo was surprised to find herself bowing deeply, as if she had been pleading on behalf of her own father.

Later that evening her brother-in-law came to her in the kitchen. He held an elaborately decorated puppet box. "This used to be Father's favorite," he whispered. "We don't do the play anymore; it won't be missed."

Once alone she removed the lid. Master Kurobe's favorite: she envisioned silk-draped nobility, or a warrior in splendid armor. Instead she discovered a meager figure in the humble clothes of an artisan, the plain face carved into an expression suggesting some sort of long-suffering endurance.

She placed it in a corner of his room, the box open so he could see what was inside. When she returned the next day the puppet was still where she'd left it. Over time it grayed with dust there in its corner. He no longer appeared to have any interest in his art. At times, though, she would enter his room to find his fingers moving, a precise kind of twitching, as if he were operating invisible controls . . .

Chiyo had always hated her father-in-law. No; that wasn't quite true—before her marriage, she could hardly believe her luck: to wed the son of the great Kurobe! She had pictured, when the marriage was arranged, a life of even greater pleasures than she had enjoyed at home; Master Kurobe was certainly far wealthier than her own father, himself a renowned musician. She had grown up pampered; under the city's finest masters, she had learned flower arranging, the tea ceremony, dance, and—her favorite of all—calligraphy. (Her calligraphy teacher once told her she was the most gifted student he'd ever taught.) At the time she'd taken it all as her due; but even if she had stopped to consider these indulgences, she would have said they were merely tokens of her parents' love; it was only later that, looking back bitterly on her life before marriage, a life that seemed to have belonged to someone else, she began to suspect that it had all been grooming—bait to attract a respectable husband. After the ceremony, her new father-in-law, regal and handsome in his wedding kimono, stood before her parents with tears in his eyes, promising to welcome Chiyo into his home as his own daughter. How her parents had groveled then, weeping and bowing and thanking him again and again!

She had imagined the Kurobe home as a temple to Beauty and Art, a place where her calligraphy, her dancing, her sense of aesthetics, everything she held true would be embraced, even applauded, by her new family. Instead the servant was let go and Chiyo given her chores. Her life before marriage had been filled with the joys of creating; the greatest creation of all, though, she realized later, had been the future she'd imagined for herself. Now her days were spent tending to three grown men and the enormous house they occupied. This alone she could perhaps have forgiven; but she couldn't forget the tender look on Master Kurobe's face as he made his promise to her parents. And since that day? He had never once treated her as even a daughter-in-law, let alone a daughter. From her first moment in the Kurobe home he was brusque, preoccupied, barely speaking except to give orders. She might have been nothing more than a new serving girl . . .

Trembling, pulling strands of wet hair from her face, she detailed for her parents between sobs (and—mysteriously— hiccups) the injustices she was suffering. Her father appeared to examine a mat's frayed edge. Her mother, finally, spoke: she should be grateful. She should be grateful to Master Kurobe.

(For a moment Chiyo was so stunned the sobs and hiccups ceased.) Master Kurobe had done only what was proper: keeping the servant on would have been an insult not only to Chiyo but to her family as well, suggesting her incapable of fulfilling her new duties as wife and daughter-in-law. Did Chiyo understand those duties? Did she understand that she had another family now? It went on and on, Chiyo receiving instead of sympathy the first severe scolding of her life: her mother, who had never once made her lift a finger at home, now demanded that she do what was expected of her without complaint.

Naturally, what was expected of her included, in due course, bearing a child. And she herself began to hope that mother-hood might bring her acceptance into the Kurobe family. On the first night of each week, with perfect regularity, her new husband appeared at her bed; there followed a fruitless inter-lude which, in the beginning, embarrassed them both. Neither spoke of it. He persevered, stoical and resolute; and this became their weekly ritual of failure. When he did succeed, it was during rare illicit visits, visits which violated his own unstated rule to share a bed only at prescribed times. She would wake to find him slipping under her covers. She tried to remain still as he held her, his grip desperate and impersonal. He seemed to have been seized himself by some unbearable force; above her he struggled against invisible snares. She lay very still. Near the end he became—not cruel exactly; but there was an off-handed roughness in his actions that suggested revulsion. She didn't know if he was disgusted with her, or with his own need of a body beneath him. When he was finished he averted his face, murmured an apology, and returned to his bed. She kept hoping that what she endured on these nights might be repaid with a child. She made a pilgrimage to Kasuga Shrine, laid an infant's pillow before the giant stone phallus, and prayed with genuine ardor for the first time in her life. She wore a fertility charm wherever she went. Still there was no child; and as the years passed she could sense Master Kurobe's indifference to her changing to something colder . . .

She had therefore come to despise her father-in-law just as she felt herself despised by him. But now that she was entrusted with his care, a new feeling came over her which grew as his mind deteriorated. It was a long time before she identified this feeling as love. Not only love, but an increasingly possessive love that astounded her. He was hers, hers completely to keep and to care for, a man turned as helpless at times as a baby. She had never experienced such joy—or any joy at all, for that matter—in ministering to someone's needs. She began to spoil him, going beyond the ordinary services she had always provided, although she knew he wouldn't appreciate or even remember her kindnesses. At the same time, she started neglecting him in small ways: she would pretend occasionally not to hear when he called for tea; or carefully undercook his food; or leave in his soup the kind of mushroom she knew he disliked; or, in the later days of his illness, allow him to sit for a while in his own filth before changing his diapers; and these too seemed, no less than any kindness she might show, a secret way of expressing her love. She felt closer to the old man than ever when she could choose whether to reward or to punish, whether to tenderly watch over him or to disregard him completely.

He called Chiyo by her name, and then he called her by his dead wife's name, and then, finally, he called her nothing at all, but merely regarded her with a look of fixed concentration. He retained a faith in himself which was now misplaced, a stubborn certainty that, even in the face of his collapse, if he concentrated hard enough he could recover his memories through force of will. His will! she thought. It was unquenched. It seemed, if anything, stronger than before, as if to make up for the other parts of himself that had fallen away. And once his will had finished searching the depleted honeycomb of his memories, buzzing desperately through the empty chambers, his rage was like nothing she'd ever seen. Only she witnessed it; his sons never came to him. It was as if they were afraid of their father, as if in his dotage he had grown in power rather than relinquishing it. (The old man, in any case, seemed to have forgotten them.) She witnessed his rage and despair alone, and suffered such unendurable pity that she felt herself wishing there were a way to spare him, even if it meant putting an end to what had become his life. Wasn't that really the kindest thing anyone could do for him now?

She began gradually, in fits and starts, to consider poisoning her father-in-law. Once she accepted that such a thing was possible the particulars seemed to unfold spontaneously like flowers into light. But then guilt would weaken her resolve, and she would question whether she would be acting to spare the old man or to spare herself, and she would refuse to think of poisoning him again until some fresh incident forced the idea back into her mind.

The worst of these incidents began with the sound of a voice rising from his room. He rarely talked to himself, and so she approached his door, listening. At first she couldn't catch his words. It was the tone of his voice: determined; authoritative. As if everything had come back to him. As if he'd been restored to his former self. And a growing impatience—the voice of a man who's come to an important decision. The voice rose:

"Oike!" he began shouting. "Where is Oike? Bring me my little man!"

It continued for what seemed like hours. The voice grew frustrated; then incensed; then anguished and desolate, while she remained where she was on the other side of the door as it jolted and shook, unable to move for fear of being heard. She was perhaps never closer than at that moment to carrying out her plan to end his life; she felt sure she could never stand to hear those shouts again.

But finally it stopped; and when, two days later, it began again, an idea came to her. A possible remedy; a way to silence his cries. It seemed monstrous; but those cries of his . . . She ran to his room and, trying it out, was astonished and even frightened to see how a few words from her could have such an effect. After that, when the voice began rising—for this had become a recurring event, sometimes happening nearly every day; other times weeks might go by before he started in again— she knew what to do. It was simple, really. And each time she did it, each time she succeeded in silencing him, the pity that had previously overwhelmed her diminished, becoming a little easier to bear.

Over time her way of looking after her father-in-law changed, as if her remedy had initiated a new phase in her relationship with him. The weakening of her love was so gradual that she barely noticed its passing; love had, in any case, been merely an aberration in her life, and she returned to her previous existence with a kind of relief. She no longer spoiled the old man, nor did she neglect him; she never felt the thrill of being unable to decide whether to reward or to punish. Caring for him became, finally, nothing but another chore, although naturally she did what was proper until the very end, continuing to provide for his needs with all of the dedication owed to him as a father-in-law.

And her remedy? The way to silence him? As stated above, it was a simple thing.

When he started calling out—"Oike! Where is Oike?"—she rushed to his room. Unbarred the door. He would be sitting there in the screened half-light, watching alertly.

"Oike is on his way, Father," she said. "He'll be here soon."

Hearing this, his face—stitched and seamed and bound together by its look of perpetual suspicion—seemed to spread open like a pouch being turned inside out. The face became radiant.

It was safe to leave then. She could go back to her chores. He wouldn't bother her anymore. He wouldn't cry out. He would be in his room with that new face of his, waiting. And it was just a matter of time, of course, before he completely forgot once again what it was he'd been waiting for.

The Involuntary Sojourner:
A Case Study

While much current research has centered on the challenges faced by international students, businesspeople, and military personnel traveling abroad, relatively little has been written about the plight of involuntary sojourners, more commonly known as "in-between people," after the name given by Takahashi in his (1996) landmark study of the subject. Both Takahashi and the author of this article, along with a number of other researchers, have since attempted to better understand the phenomenon through an interdisciplinary approach drawing on various fields including intercultural psychology, anthropology, and communication theory; nevertheless, Involuntary Sojourning Syndrome (ISS) remains elusive and is perhaps best examined through the lens of some new, as yet nonexistent, field of study. This article will attempt to address deficiencies in existing research through an investigation into the case of a single "in-between person."

Takahashi has defined the involuntary sojourner as one who "finds him/herself abruptly and inexplicably abroad, without any prior intent to travel or knowledge regarding how s/he arrived in the host culture" (1996, 185). The first known occurrence of "in-betweenness" concerned a subject who came to be pseudonymously referred to as "Shin." Shin's case—that of a thirty-nine-year-old Japanese male discovered wandering "trancelike" in a repeating figure-eight pattern through the aisles of a Brittany souvenir shop specializing in reproductions of locally famous painted dishware—was widely reported by the media and caused a brief international stir as a result of the diplomatic row between Japan and France regarding his status (France asserting that Shin had violated the implied conditions of the tourist visa issued since he had not entered the country "by free and conscious choice"), but has since been eclipsed by the numerous other cases which have proliferated in the intervening years. Takahashi's study ignored the sensational aspects of the case, focusing instead on the problems of culture shock and adaptation experienced by Shin in his new situation. Linguistic issues, often a concern for sojourners, were found not to be relevant in Shin's case, since he reportedly possessed, at least for the duration of his stay in Brittany, native-like fluency in French despite having never studied the language (an assertion later corroborated by Delavergne & Arbogast, 1997). This study, in spite of its unavoidable limitations and remaining questions, constituted an important first step in the understanding of "in-between people."

(It is worth noting that Takahashi himself, in private correspondence with the author, has confided his dissatisfaction with the term "in-between," considering it a poor translation of the Japanese word *chuto-hanpa*, which connotes an insufficiency, a sense of being stranded between poles, which is ultimately untranslatable, but perhaps better captured, according to Takahashi, by the colloquial English term "half-assed." For understandable reasons, however, the term "half-assed people" has not been adopted by those pursuing this research. [The author will not address here the other issue regarding nomenclature, which involves the use of the term "involuntary" with respect to these sojourners (see Pflogg, 2007, for an amusingly misguided discussion of this question). Suffice to say that although, as Pflogg states sardonically, it is true that the involuntary sojourner "does not simply materialize in the host country: he purchases the tickets; he boards the plane; finding his seat, he makes himself comfortable and fastens his seat belt when instructed to do so; he from all reports avails himself of the snacks and meal included and in one case even requests an alcoholic beverage; he presumably selects from among the in-flight entertainment provided; he presents his passport to an immigration official upon arrival; and, leaving the airport, he even hails a taxi" (Pflogg, 2007, 41), this does not in any way constitute proof that those afflicted with "in-betweenness" are necessarily aware of what they are doing, or why. Thus "involuntary." Unless one wishes to go so far as to dispute the amnesia or blocked memory itself as hoax, a position even Pflogg hesitates to take openly, though his article is rife with cunningly worded innuendo to this effect. (As an aside, Pflogg's above litany of behavior "proving" volition conveniently omits one significant detail: in no case has a sojourner brought a single carry-on bag to stow in the overhead bin; neither has there ever been a single case of checked luggage or any other sign of the preparation one would reasonably expect if travel were in fact deliberately planned. The corpus amply demonstrates that the involuntary sojourner acts without choosing to act, behaves with intent but without conscious volition, in a manner superficially similar to but in fact distinct from psychotic compulsion [Takahashi & Kalvan, 2004; Kalvan, Beebe, Hardwick & Wendt-McCruthers, 2007; Kalvan & Nightingale, 2010].)])

This study will examine a single subject using both objective evaluative measures and self-reported material in the form of a journal kept by the subject (hereafter "L") concerning her experiences. L, a twenty-seven-year-old U.S. national, was discovered in the home appliance section of a department store in the commercial district of Vivasha, Gandarva's largest city, her motion describing what has come to be known as a "Takahashi Loop," i.e., the now familiar figure-eight pattern representing a closed loop interrupted only when the subject is addressed or physically restrained, usually by shop clerk or official, at which point the somnambulant sojourner, if we can use such a term (see Balbain, 2010, for an intriguing if speculative consideration of possible sleep-associated delta wave activity in ISS trance states), "wakes up," becoming cognizant of his or her surroundings.

The author was subsequently contacted by the U.S. Department of State and asked to provide consultation in the case. This presented an exciting and unprecedented opportunity: although the author had interviewed and evaluated a large number of involuntary sojourners while conducting previous research, this always occurred following the return to home countries, at which point the subjects, it was found, retained only "dreamlike" fragments of the episodes. The Gandarvan government allowed the author access to L, at the time being detained pending resolution of her case, on the condition that he accept responsibility for her care until her return to the United States. (One must note briefly here the evident relief with which this responsibility was transferred; the local doctors, including several "experts" in atypical psychosis, appeared to be completely unfamiliar with ISS. The various diagnostic reports provided to the author were useful only insofar as they offered particularly dramatic examples of the need for greater education regarding the syndrome.)

ENTRY I

So Victor's asked me to keep this journal. He said it'll be useful in his research into in-between people. I want to help—Victor's very persuasive in his sort of weirdly intense way, sorry Victor I know you'll be reading this but you asked me to tell the truth—I want to help but I don't think there's anything "in-between" about my situation. I'm here. Here being Gandarva, they tell me. It's not like I'm in between countries. Here I am. In this room provided by the Gandarvan government, who keep telling me I'm not under arrest even though I can't leave. They keep using the word "policy" and smiling. A guy from the U.S. consulate or embassy or someplace came today. He was smiling too. Everybody's smiling. Not as in trying-not-to-laugh smiling, but as in . . . As in what? Even Victor smiles at me all the time. Everybody's so happy for me, like I've just been given an award. So this U.S. consulate or embassy guy comes in. He wants me to call him Tom. He looks a little young to be a diplomat. He's wearing a traditional *pulcha*, rows of bright triangles alternating with upside-down triangles, he's even got the knot at his hip tied the right way. He tells me this is the first case in this country so it's still a little thorny, that's his word, thorny, which makes me think, what about this other word "policy" that keeps getting thrown around, if there's a policy in place why the thorns? But he says he's confident, what with international precedent, that this case, my case, can be cleared up and I can return home soon.

Home?

The reader's attention is directed to L's knowledge in the above entry regarding specific details of traditional Gandarvan clothing; this appears to be symptomatic of the Kalvan Effect (so named by other researchers, one is quick to point out; in the author's view the effect should rightfully have been given Takahashi's name to honor his brilliant and pioneering work in the subject). The phenomenon, peculiar to the involuntary sojourner, can be described as "unexplained familiarity . . . with previously unknown elements of the host culture" (Kalvan, 2008, 73). In short, involuntary sojourners know things they have no apparent way of knowing, without the slightest idea as to how they came to possess this knowledge.

(As the informed reader will no doubt already be aware, the Kalvan Effect is not to be confused with the so-called "Kalvan Affect." The author recalls vividly his first encounter with the term, in a 2009 Pflogg monograph. This was no innocuous typographical error, one discovered with incredulity upon further reading; it was, rather, an attack: concocted by Pflogg, the term reflected his assertion, without the tiniest scrap of supporting evidence, that any claimed "magical" knowledge constitutes an act, an affectation [therefore "Affect"], essentially premeditated falsification, the sojourner having in fact obtained the pertinent information regarding the target culture in advance. This argument, modified later to include "inadvertent falsification" [Pflogg, 2010, 45], i.e., the drawing on information in fact learned but later forgotten, having been buried in the subconscious, has been more than adequately refuted elsewhere [see Kalvan, 2011] and will therefore not be addressed in this article except to reiterate that the nature and extent of the involuntary sojourner's knowledge, whether sociolinguistic, geographic, or other, far exceeds what would be possible if the subject had simply conducted surreptitious research prior to travel. Is it even worth mentioning that the term "Kalvan Affect" additionally constitutes a baseless and puerile attack upon the author himself, suggesting either deliberate exaggeration of the phenomenon for professional advancement or, at the very least, credulousness, a case of "taking a subject's claims at face value without adequate corroboration or independent verification" [Pflogg, 2009, 53]?)

To return to the above journal entry, L's suspicion toward those attempting to help her has not been reported in other cases and may reflect preexisting individual cognitive style (i.e., her "personality") rather than being symptomatic of ISS post-loop behavioral shift. While the author cannot presume to speak for the others involved in this case, the author himself was, as should be clear, simply employing a well-established prosocial display signal (viz., "smiling") in an effort to reassure the subject and alleviate the altogether understandable stress engendered by her predicament (see, for instance, Moynihan et al., 1999, for a study of the efficacy of positive facial expression in crisis tension relief).

ENTRY 2

There's a window in my room. No bars or anything, but on the other hand it can't be opened either. I'm standing with

my hands against the glass when Tom bounces in, all spry and
dapper in a blue suit. Hi, he says.

Hi.

Not thinking of jumping, are you? he says, smile increasing
fractionally for contrast.

I point out that there's no way to open it, and that the glass
looks like it's at least five centimeters thick. Inches, I mean.
Two inches thick.

When did I ever use the metric system?

Outside the window is a view of a hill. I recognize it,
even though I shouldn't. Go over the top of the hill and
there's the place where they have the Saturday market under
a tilting network of tarps and rusted poles, half-bald ribby
dogs weaving in their perpetual loops through stalls full of
hand-carved good-luck charms, plastic toys made in China,
fish hanging from strings, knockoff electronic goods, *tolten*
in varying stages of decay. I shouldn't know any of this either.
I've never been there.

I want to ask Tom where his *pulcha* is. And then I want
to tell him that nobody wears *pulchas* anymore and that he
looked ridiculous, but the truth is he looks more ridiculous in
his fancy blue suit. He looks like a boy on his first job interview.

Good news, he says: the authorities have decided to let you
leave this room. You can stay at the consulate. I guess that
means the thorns have all been picked out of the policy, I
say. Nicely put, Tom says, but he's not smiling anymore. He
tells me I can move freely within the city until the matter
is resolved and I'm allowed to return home. How long will
that be? Oh, shouldn't be long, Tom says. Professor Kalvan
has agreed to assist in my case. Which I guess means escort.

Guard. So much for "moving freely." Oh well. At least I'll be out of this room.

L was subsequently relocated to the U.S. consulate while awaiting the final resolution of her case including the issuance of travel documents.

ENTRY 3

Victor gives me a test. He says it's used to "measure readjustment in sojourners" after they arrive in a foreign country. He doesn't leave while I take the test, which makes me nervous. And he wears this cologne . . . (Sorry Victor.) He won't explain the test. Or he says he'll explain the test questions if I can't understand them but that I'm on my own as far as answering . . .

The results of the Fochner-Kline Intercultural Adaptation Survey referenced above indicated self-construal redefinition within the normal parameters observed in voluntary sojourners following transition from home to host culture. No indicators of psychiatric morbidity resulting from adaptation failure were present. Assimilation anxiety was a negligible 0.07. The subject's integrative orientation score, however, ordinarily associated with field independence and robust acculturation potential in voluntary sojourners, was an unexpectedly high 44.3. The author does not wear cologne. The comment may represent (a) phantom olfactory input, which would constitute a new characteristic of the condition meriting future study; (b) masked aggression toward the researcher, possibly due to psychological stress related to test-taking; or (c) unusual sensitivity to the author's inoffensive musk aftershave lotion.

ENTRY 4

Victor's sitting across from me on a chair in the consulate. He asks me if I remember being in the department store. He looks tired and excited at the same time. Of course I remember. He asks me if I remember making figure eights through the aisles. No. Do I remember anything before that? No. Booking the flight to this country? Getting on the plane? Arriving here? No, no, and no.

I tell him I need fresh air. Not that it's exactly fresh out there. Some places stink worse than others, though. The stink is familiar, but that doesn't necessarily mean anything. Stink is stink, right?

I go through alleys. Down streets. Up hills. It's not like I know where I'm going. I just . . . People stare from doorways, windows. They don't recognize me. Well, why should they? I don't know what I mean. Victor's finding it hard to keep up. Are you leading me somewhere or trying to ditch me? he asks irritably, sweaty and out of breath.

Neither one, I say. I keep walking.

What's it like? he says behind me.

What's what like?

He jogs to catch up, backpack jiggling and jouncing.

This. His hand waves around, at the side of a building, at sun on sidewalk. Knowing . . . (He's really out of breath.)

I don't know anything. I'm just walking, I say. And that's what I do—I walk. After a minute I hear him behind me, swearing softly to himself, jingling and jouncing.

It is necessary to interject here; despite L's comments to the contrary, her movements displayed clear purpose and evident knowledge of her at times labyrinthine surroundings. The author, frankly, ended up completely lost; L, however, after completing a tour of commonplace objects and buildings which she stopped to study intently, was able, without apparent effort, to find a way back to the consulate (the author following as best he could) via a circuitous path through back streets, over rubble, across footbridges, past the inverted gold cups of temple domes, without once consulting map or digital navigation device.

ENTRY 5

I live in A—— with my sister. My older sister K——. Who must be wondering what the hell is going on. Along with everyone else in my family. They've been contacted, Tom tells me. But not by me. Not yet. I've finally been allowed to make calls, but I haven't gotten to it yet. I'm waiting for (illegible) . . . (*Author's note: The previous sentence was written and then erased, but remained visible on the page, and is therefore being recorded here.*)

I'm twenty-seven years old. I graduated from A—— State with a major in economics, don't ask me why. I've been working for the last two years as a temp at an operations research firm, again don't ask why. I've never been to Gandarva before. Never studied the language or anything. Until now it was a name, a place on a map. I didn't even know about the earthquake here until Tom told me all about it in gory detail.

There. Satisfied, Victor? No amnesia. That's who I am, that's where I'm from. Except for the one thing I put in there that isn't true. Just to fuck with you. Consider it a puzzle. Or a gift. Just don't consider it a symptom of involuntary sojourning or whatever you call it.

One must at this point raise the possibility that the entries are designed not to enlighten the researcher but rather to frustrate any attempt to understand the phenomenon under consideration. As seen above, at least some of the comments appear to be indicative of withholding, if not intentional misleading, and seem calculated to irritate or perhaps even enrage the author, to force him to abandon his neutral stance and fall into the mire of intersubjectivity. L's obstructive behavior may suggest negative transference, normally encountered in the psychiatrist/patient dyad, but not without precedent in researcher/subject relations (Kilgatten, 1978; Pool, 1985). In any event, it is clear that L is making every effort to further obscure a subject which can already seem unfathomable, which, at times apparently and delusively near, proceeds to move away ever more quickly the more one pursues it . . . What is the real internal state of the involuntary sojourner? One is confronted by the limits of self-reporting, of qualitative research in general, when attempting to capture, or rather grasp, or rather understand this subject, difficult enough to penetrate without willful (and one might almost be inclined to say malicious) obfuscation on L's part . . .

The author observes at times an expression on her face . . . She notices herself being observed. The author attempts a smile; since reading her comment regarding smiling, however, the author has found himself becoming so self-conscious that the smile may well have the qualities of muscles being pulled mechanically into place or even of a grimace. We face one another, L with her undefinable expression and the author with his smile which no longer feels consistent with anything Moynihan et al. have advocated as efficacious in crisis tension relief . . .

ENTRY 6

I lead Victor to a restaurant. I'm craving *bujya*. An old woman shows us to a table. Once we're seated Victor asks me if I'm aware of the fact that I've just spoken to her in Gandarvan. I ask him what he's talking about. He nods, holds his palm out in front of me, pulls notebook out of backpack and starts scribbling . . .

Then he seems to remember that he has a recorder with him and asks if he can record our conversation.

What conversation? I ask.

What I mean is, assuming we . . . Our dinner conversation, he says. If it's all right.

It's not all right, I say. We're here to eat. Now look at your menu.

You don't eat it that way, I tell him when the food comes. You tear the *pakla* leaf with your left hand before scooping up the rice. I'm expecting him to be embarrassed, which he should be, but he sits up straight and asks if I know how I know that. I learned it from a waiter in a Gandarvan restaurant, I say. Back in the U.S. Don't get too excited, I say. He looks disappointed.

But I found it really embarrassing, I tell him. Which I don't think I would have in America.

He looks doubtful.

You're being kind, he says. But this is research. Don't throw me any bones, please.

Sorry, I say. And we don't talk about it anymore. Victor sits there brooding, or something. Not touching his food. He doesn't look so good.

But hey Victor? I really *did* find it embarrassing. Maybe that's something for you, something you can use.

The author watched L dine with gusto and, one assumes, impeccable table manners (as the above entry makes clear, the author is apparently unfit to judge the niceties of Gandarvan etiquette); then, having unfortunately lost his appetite, excused himself. As of this writing, the day after the above entry, the author has been experiencing for a week gastrointestinal discomfort together with a general malaise and intermittent low-grade fever, denoting either a microbial infection or, conceivably, a somatic condition caused by the unexpected challenges arising from the current research. The author has, however, avoided seeking medical care, due to (1) doubts regarding the level of care in this country; and (2) fears that any required hospitalization might interrupt his research. In any event, as the informed reader will know, the field of cross-cultural studies is littered with firsthand accounts of the difficulties faced by sojourners encountering the bewildering variety of seatless (and often alarmingly unsanitary) toilet facilities found in "non-Western" host cultures. It is only through direct experience, however, that one fully comprehends the often-described gratitude experienced upon opening a restroom door and being greeted by that familiar and previously unappreciated porcelain sign of home. Once seated, one wishes, almost, to remain there . . .

On the restroom's opposite wall was a painting. Goddesses, or bodhisattvas, or possibly angels, or in any case spiritual beings of some sort, a dozen of them, floated above a lily-spotted pond. Some held the slender stalks of flowers in slender fingers; others, flowerless, displayed instead flames burning on upheld palms. They had no legs, or perhaps their legs were folded beneath flowing dresses that might also have been blue-green tails. They floated there in the middle of the painting, above lily pads and below mottled sky, gold-silhouetted, smirking at one another in a collusion of ecstasy.

The author reached down to his ankled trousers, fished in a

pocket, found his keys, rose, shuffled across the tiled floor, and, scraping away at the paint, etched a cartoon thought bubble so that it floated there too, over one of the shining heads. Inside the bubble, the author scratched the words IN BETWEEN. Keys were returned to pocket, removed again; at the bottom of the painting, in the right corner, the author scrawled PFLOGG.

ENTRY 7

So my case has been "resolved." I can go home. Victor asked me if I was homesick. We were at the Saturday market.

Are you asking that in your professional capacity? I said.

He seemed confused by the question. He stood there, turning a half-ripe mango in his hands.

I mean, is that part of your research?

I was curious, he said. Homesickness is an expected part of the sojourn experience.

With us too? I said.

Us? . . . You mean involuntary sojourners?

Yeah. Us in-between people, I said. (I've started to like the name, by the way. In-between people.)

Well, the results are inconclusive . . . He picked up a plastic action figure.

Baku-baku chan, I told him. An anime character. It was big when I was a kid. She can like turn herself into a bomb. A love bomb. Hearts everywhere. She explodes and everyone stops fighting.

He set it down. Obviously, there's individual variation. And even if you . . . I can't assume, I don't want you to think you're necessarily representative of all involuntary sojourners, he said.

You said.

I don't know if I'm even representative of me, I said.

I'm writing this so you'll remember it Victor. In case you weren't recording everything secretly.

Oh. Don't try to pet the dogs. I meant to tell you that at the market. I wish I could have helped. With whatever it is you needed from me. Good luck.

This was to be L's final entry. But we may as well dispense here with pseudonyms. "L" is gone; she was in a sense never there. She is Lauren. Let her be Lauren then. Shortly after the exchange recorded above—by "recorded," the author is referring to Lauren's own journal entry; naturally the author had not, for both ethical and legal reasons, recorded conversations without permission—Lauren disappeared. The author learned of this through a phone call received in his hotel room. The consulate, hoping to forestall the troubles which, it was felt, would inevitably arise if the Gandarvan government became aware of her disappearance, were conducting their own discreet search. It was believed that she was still in the country—her financial resources were limited, and consular officials were in possession of her passport. As the author, seated on the bed's edge, alternately winding and unwinding telephone cord around index finger, explained repeatedly to the voice on the other end of the line that he had no idea of her whereabouts, he found himself wondering: were there, in the journal entries, foreshadowings of what was to occur, warnings ignored, clues—possibly even deliberately planted but in some manner encrypted—to where she might have gone? . . .

These thoughts, these doubts, had not abated when, an hour later, the author entered her room at the consulate, having been allowed in by an official who promptly disappeared. Her journal was found on the desk, open to the final entry. Had she left it that way, as a kind of letter to the author? Or were consular officials the ones who had left it open there after searching the journal for information? The author read her final entry a number of times—good luck; good luck—and then proceeded to reread the entire journal. Finally it was closed and placed in the author's backpack. Her bed was small and (one discovered upon reclining) rather uncomfortable. I wish I could have helped, she'd written. With whatever it is you needed from me. The ceiling plaster described patterns—lakes, isthmuses, tributaries; islands and peninsulas. Would she have seen these, noticed the same patterns, the same topography, as she lay staring upward as the author was doing?

Tom the diplomat, shirtless, traditionally skirted, sandaled, swept into the room. He glanced over at the author, supine on the bed. A blue smear of paint transected his otherwise unlined forehead.

"Right," he said, crossing palms over chest in perfunctory Gandarvan greeting. "Her disappearance." He leaned against the desk. "Worries aside—I'm worried, you're worried, I think it's safe to say we're all worried—it's a little thorny is the word I want. Professor Kalvan? Are you listening?"

The author asked whether it was possible that Tom was in the habit of overusing the word "thorny." Alternatives were suggested.

"Professor, you are a regular walking thesaurus," he said. "Very professorial. Which don't think for a minute I don't appreciate it, but is now the time would be my question. When the situation is less than ideal. Your situation, I mean. When I say 'situation' I mean the responsibility you've taken with respect to our compatriot. Or how the government here might interpret said responsibility. I mean, look, she's not a child. You're not her chaperone. Et cetera. It would be nice, Professor, to feel I have your undivided attention. The situation being what it is. A ball having been dropped. Which I say with all due respect and without finger-pointing. And she may still turn up. Or she will turn up, one way or the other. She may have gone on a little excursion. Unplanned. Seeing the sights. We can hope. Or maybe we'll find her, safe and sound, or safe at least, wandering the aisles of that department store again. Perfect for us, in a way. Professor?"

Why has there, until now, never been an incident such as this, a case of a subject "going native," to borrow the term used by Tom the diplomat during the monologue which followed, the words emerging briefly from the clutter of distant noise that his monologue had otherwise become? One need look no further, perhaps, than the constant official scrutiny focused on the involuntary sojourner once discovered, scrutiny which would make slipping away into the host culture a near impossibility. Perhaps, given the opportunity, every involuntary sojourner would have behaved as Lauren did; perhaps the uniqueness of her case was due to nothing other than the "dropped ball" with respect to adequate supervision on the part of those (e.g., the author) responsible for her care. Unimpeded, does the process of involuntary sojourning end in complete integration, in a final merging with the culture to which a subject has been irresistibly drawn? Although one can't avoid suspecting that Lauren's disappearance was more, that it amounted to an attempt on her part to leave the author stranded mid-research, to deny him an opportunity to finally understand "in-betweenness." Once again, the subject of a decade of the author's professional life moves away; this time, however, out of sight altogether.

(Offering those researchers, or one might as well say researcher, in the singular, by which the author is referring of course to Pflogg, offering him a marvelous gift in his efforts to discredit the author and his work.) Of course, her disappearance may have had nothing to do with the author. It is difficult, though, to imagine such a thing happening, for instance, to Takahashi; difficult to imagine him being called "weirdly intense" by a subject under his care; difficult to envision his aftershave lotion or smile receiving criticism. Takahashi's smile the author found quite disarming when they finally met at a conference in Vancouver. Affable, tall, loose-limbed, full-bearded, Takahashi in the flesh was quite unlike the image one had formed of the man based on his written work. (Although isn't that always the case?) The author approached him tentatively following his presentation, due in part to his formidable reputation, but also in part to concerns regarding a possible language barrier: Takahashi had presented entirely in Japanese, aided by a translator; all of his research over the years had been originally written in that language as well. His near-fluency in mellifluously British-accented English (not to mention the vigorous handshake in place of the expected bow) therefore took the author by surprise. This conversation, the one and only time the author and Takahashi actually met in person, led eventually to the collaborative effort *Methodological issues in the investigation and analysis of Involuntary Sojourning Syndrome: An interdisciplinary perspective* (2004), carried out long-distance via online correspondence.

Was all of this somewhere in the author's mind when he named Tokyo, spontaneously and seemingly at random, as his destination later that afternoon at the airport ticket counter? There were no more direct flights to the U.S. that day (which is to say today), and the author was impatient to leave the country as soon as possible after the meeting with Tom the diplomat and his menacing talk of responsibility. (Could the presence of soldiers lounging with their semiautomatic weapons near the magazine kiosk have also played a subliminal role?) Still, other destinations must have been available, destinations bringing him closer to his familiar world rather than in the opposite direction. When one finds oneself suddenly presenting behavior consistent with the DSM-IV criteria for panic disorder, or possibly instead symptoms of delirium caused by the bacterial or viral infection which the author suspects has been plaguing him almost since his arrival, it becomes difficult to assess accurately one's own intentions, however much one tries as one sits here in the departures terminal, hurriedly typing these words and hoping they are coherent while awaiting the boarding call for the flight to Tokyo. Certainly, there is a curious sense that the impulse to leave comes from outside oneself rather than from within, as if this country itself is, whether through induced panic or microbial invasion, expelling the author, casting him out, a foreign body being purged by the Gandarvan immune system . . .

Is this what the in-between people experience: a simultaneous sense of being cast out and drawn in as they make the journey from home to host culture that they can later never recall?

One is tempted here to write ENTRY 1. The subject, which is to say me, or rather I, I could be Subject 2, or if Lauren were changed in the article above to Participant A, I could become Participant B. Or VK. Or simply V. (I'm too tired at the moment to devise a pseudonym.)

Any minute now the boarding call. I will board the plane. I'll behave normally. I'll find my seat, make myself comfortable, fasten my seat belt when instructed, avail myself of peanuts and let's say penne pasta Bolognese and even request a glass of wine; I'll choose two or three films from among the in-flight entertainment provided; I'll present my passport to an immigration official upon arrival; leaving Narita airport, I'll hail a taxi. (Let Pflogg sue me for plagiarism.) On the ride into Tokyo I'll think of Lauren: What was she thinking on her own taxi ride into Vivasha? *Was* she thinking? How does one render oneself into a trance state? Or can one be in a trance state already without realizing it? Can actions, seemingly conscious and deliberate, in fact be the product of an impulse one can't understand? Or would one only be pretending? "To pretend, I actually do the thing: I have therefore only pretended to pretend." Whose words? Foucault's? Derrida's? Pflogg's? I can provide no citation at the moment. No name, no year, no page number . . .

Then out of the taxi, lugging luggage. Or wait: no: no luggage—I've left it behind in the Vivasha hotel room, too late now. Any minute the boarding call. I've embarked (voluntarily?) on this sojourn without luggage, with only my "jingling and jouncing" backpack.

Out of the taxi then, having been dropped off on a random street. Is that what they do, the in-between people: choose a random location? Or is their destination predetermined, according to rules, forces, principles they needn't understand? Around me office buildings perhaps. Tokyo after all. Through windows I'll see workers at desks, segmented into vertical strips by ivory blinds. I'll walk.

To walk without purpose. To find your purpose in the walking . . .

The sky will gray, clear, gray again. People will pass through glass doors. Then I'll be inside as well.

To actually do the thing, I pretend: I have therefore only pretended to actually do the thing.

A woman (in a lemon-colored uniform?) will bow and say something—a greeting—as I enter. Will I know what she's saying? Will the Kalvan Effect come to the rescue? I will bow in return; or maybe not; whichever I do, it will be right; or she'll smile, or rather smirk, a momentary flaw, an instant of failure in the composure of her face, informing me of my faux pas.

Then aisles. Jewelry. Accessories. Escalator. More aisles. Handbags. To pretend to pretend. Children's clothing. Where do I stop? Will I know?

The sporting goods section, let's say. As good a place as any. Fishing rods, lures, I-don't-know-what. I've never been a fisherman. The fish would pound and paddle at my feet, flapping silver things beating themselves against the duller silver of my grandfather's boat, their flapping at the same time desperate and mechanical . . . I wasn't allowed to throw them back . . .

The boarding call. No more time.

The Takahashi Loop is a figure-eight pattern representing a closed loop, interrupted only when the involuntary sojourner, passing hooks, nets, fishing vests, is addressed or physically restrained—by Takahashi himself perhaps, come to pursue his research, to take his new subject away, at which point—final boarding call—at which point, pattern disturbed, the subject wakes up, becoming

S. P. TENHOFF's writing has appeared in *Conjunctions,* the *Gettysburg Review, American Short Fiction,* the *Southern Review,* the *Antioch Review, Ninth Letter, Electric Literature's Recommended Reading,* and elsewhere, and has been excerpted on Longform.org. He is a recipient of the Editor's Reprint Award and Columbia University's Bennett Cerf Memorial Prize for Fiction. His short fiction has been selected as a finalist for the Italo Calvino Prize in Fabulist Fiction, among other awards. The Involuntary Sojourner was a finalist for the Mary McCarthy Prize and the Autumn House Fiction Prize.

SEVEN STORIES PRESS is an independent book publisher based in New York City. We publish works of the imagination by such writers as Nelson Algren, Russell Banks, Octavia E. Butler, Ani DiFranco, Assia Djebar, Ariel Dorfman, Coco Fusco, Barry Gifford, Martha Long, Luis Negrón, Peter Plate, Hwang Sok-yong, Lee Stringer, and Kurt Vonnegut, to name a few, together with political titles by voices of conscience, including Subhankar Banerjee, the Boston Women's Health Collective, Noam Chomsky, Angela Y. Davis, Human Rights Watch, Derrick Jensen, Ralph Nader, Loretta Napoleoni, Gary Null, Greg Palast, Project Censored, Barbara Seaman, Alice Walker, Gary Webb, and Howard Zinn, among many others. Seven Stories Press believes publishers have a special responsibility to defend free speech and human rights, and to celebrate the gifts of the human imagination, wherever we can. In 2012 we launched Triangle Square books for young readers with strong social justice and narrative components, telling personal stories of courage and commitment. For additional information, visit www.sevenstories.com.